A LUCKY LUKE ADVENTURE

ON THE DALTONS' TRAIL

BY MORRIS & GOSCINNY

Original title: Lucky Luke – Sur la piste des Dalton

Original edition: © Dargaud Editeur Paris 1971 by Goscinny and Morris
© Lucky Comics
www.lucky-luke.com

English translation: © 2009 Cinebook Ltd

Translator: Luke Spear
Lettering and text layout: Imadjinn sarl
Printed in Spain by Just Colour Graphic

This edition first published in Great Britain in 2009 by
Cinebook Ltd
56 Beech Avenue
Canterbury, Kent
CT4 7TA
www.cinebook.com

A CIP catalogue record for this book
is available from the British Library

ISBN 978-1-84918-007-8

9th CINEBOOK
The 9th Art Publisher

ON THE DALTONS' TRAIL

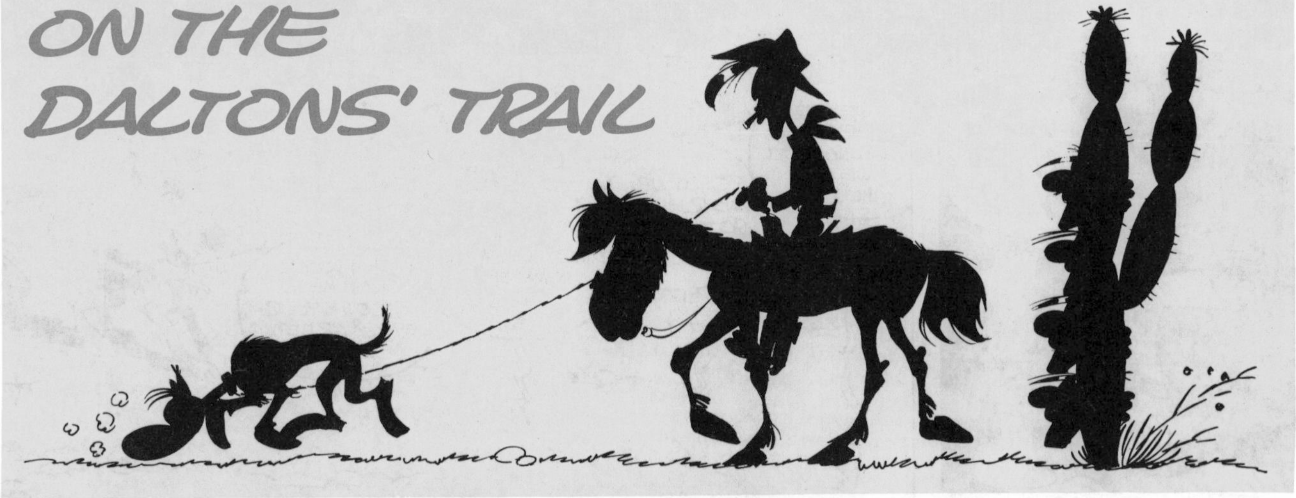

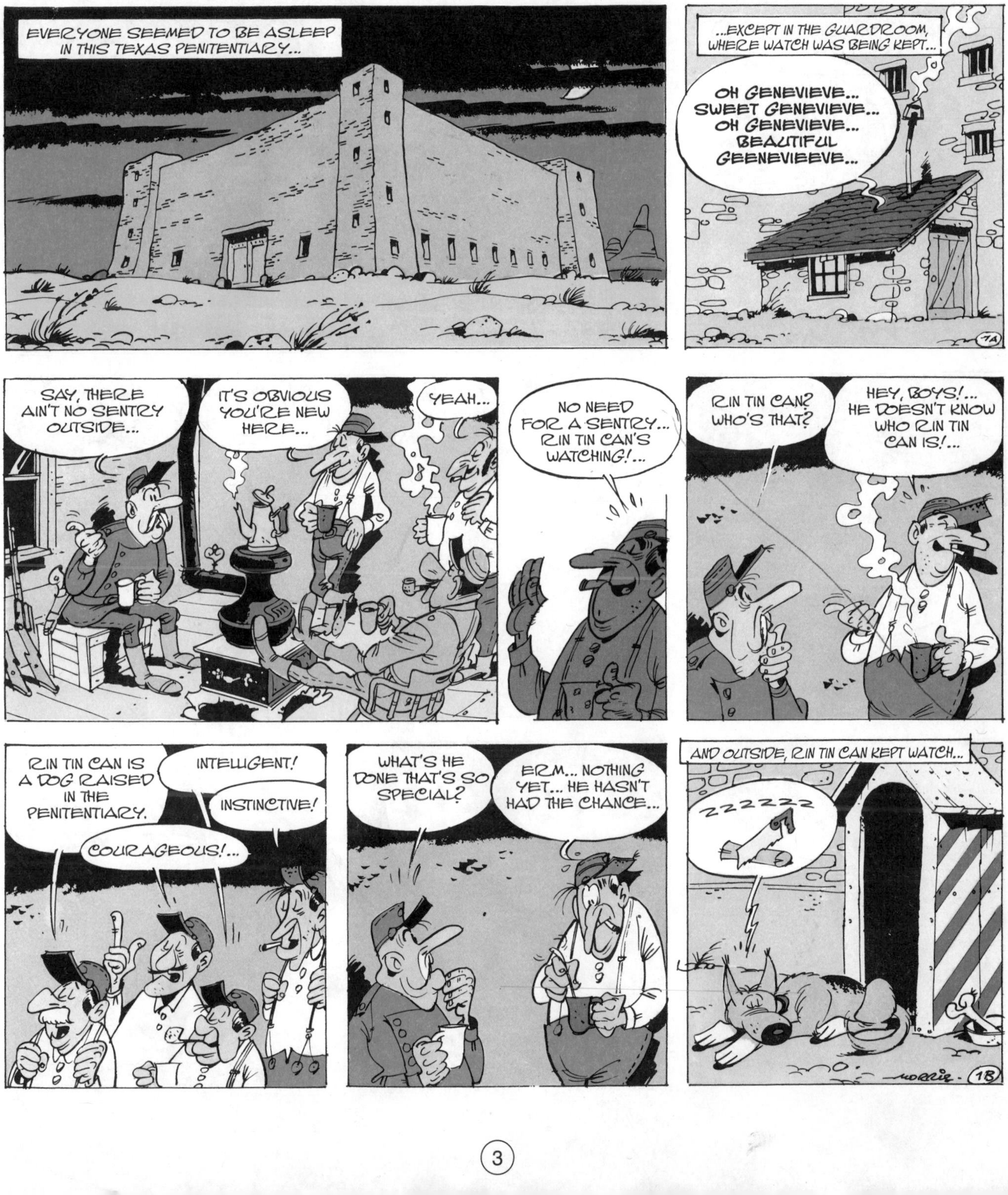

EVERYONE SEEMED TO BE ASLEEP IN THIS TEXAS PENITENTIARY...
...EXCEPT IN THE GUARDROOM, WHERE WATCH WAS BEING KEPT...
OH GENEVIEVE... SWEET GENEVIEVE... OH GENEVIEVE... BEAUTIFUL GEENEVIEEVE...
SAY, THERE AIN'T NO SENTRY OUTSIDE...
IT'S OBVIOUS YOU'RE NEW HERE...
YEAH...
NO NEED FOR A SENTRY... RIN TIN CAN'S WATCHING!...
RIN TIN CAN? WHO'S THAT?
HEY, BOYS!... HE DOESN'T KNOW WHO RIN TIN CAN IS!...
RIN TIN CAN IS A DOG RAISED IN THE PENITENTIARY.
INTELLIGENT!
INSTINCTIVE!
COURAGEOUS!...
WHAT'S HE DONE THAT'S SO SPECIAL?
ERM... NOTHING YET... HE HASN'T HAD THE CHANCE...
AND OUTSIDE, RIN TIN CAN KEPT WATCH...
ZZZZZZ
MORRIS

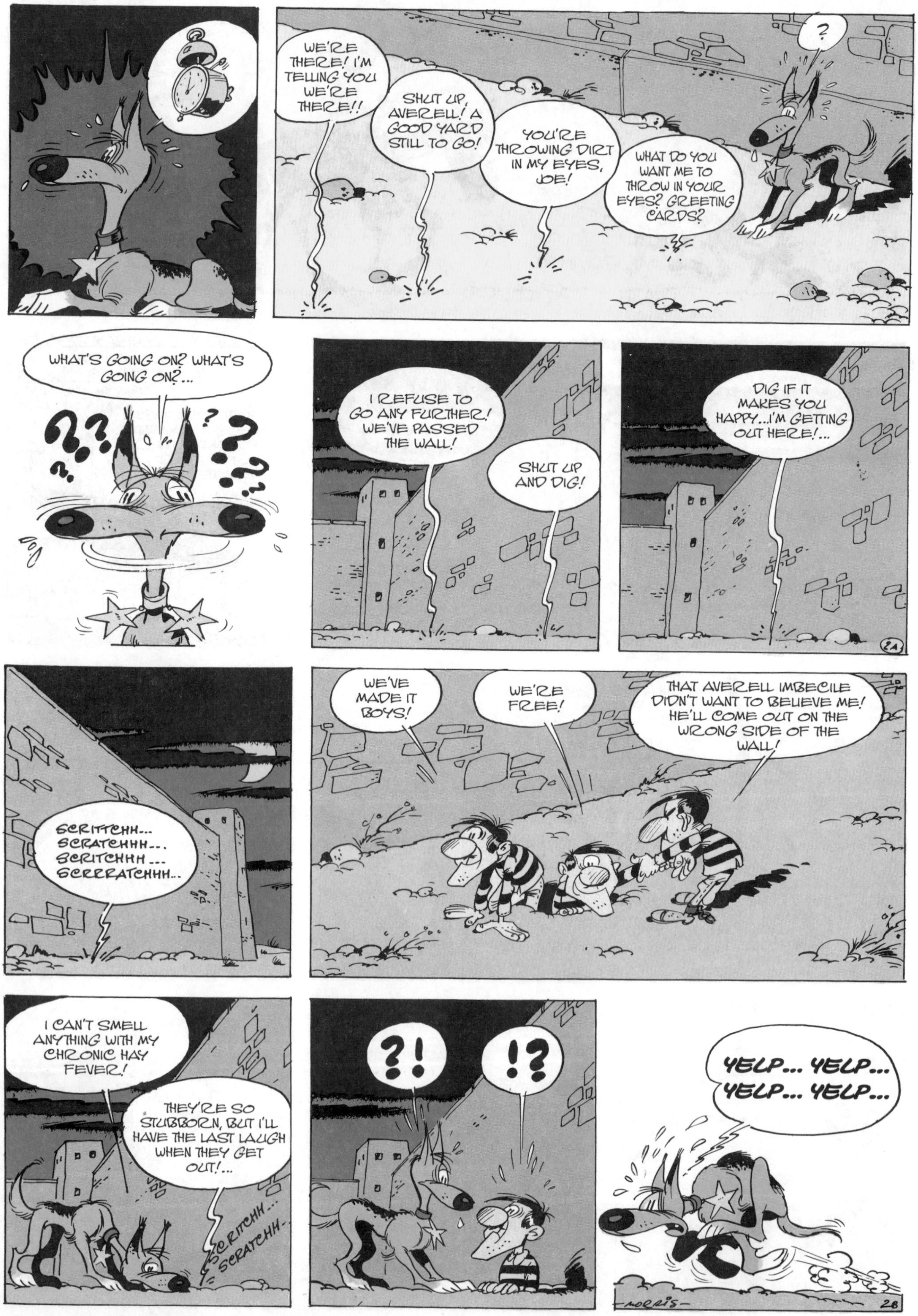
WE'RE THERE! I'M TELLING YOU WE'RE THERE!!
SHUT UP, AVERELL! A GOOD YARD STILL TO GO!
YOU'RE THROWING DIRT IN MY EYES, JOE!
WHAT DO YOU WANT ME TO THROW IN YOUR EYES? GREETING CARDS?
?
WHAT'S GOING ON? WHAT'S GOING ON?...
I REFUSE TO GO ANY FURTHER! WE'VE PASSED THE WALL!
SHUT UP AND DIG!
DIG IF IT MAKES YOU HAPPY...I'M GETTING OUT HERE!...
SCRITTCHH... SCRATCHHH... SCRITCHHH... SCRRRATCHHH...
WE'VE MADE IT BOYS!
WE'RE FREE!
THAT AVERELL IMBECILE DIDN'T WANT TO BELIEVE ME! HE'LL COME OUT ON THE WRONG SIDE OF THE WALL!
I CAN'T SMELL ANYTHING WITH MY CHRONIC HAY FEVER!
THEY'RE SO STUBBORN, BUT I'LL HAVE THE LAST LAUGH WHEN THEY GET OUT!...
SCRITCHH... SCRATCHH...
?!
!?
YELP... YELP... YELP... YELP...
MORRIS

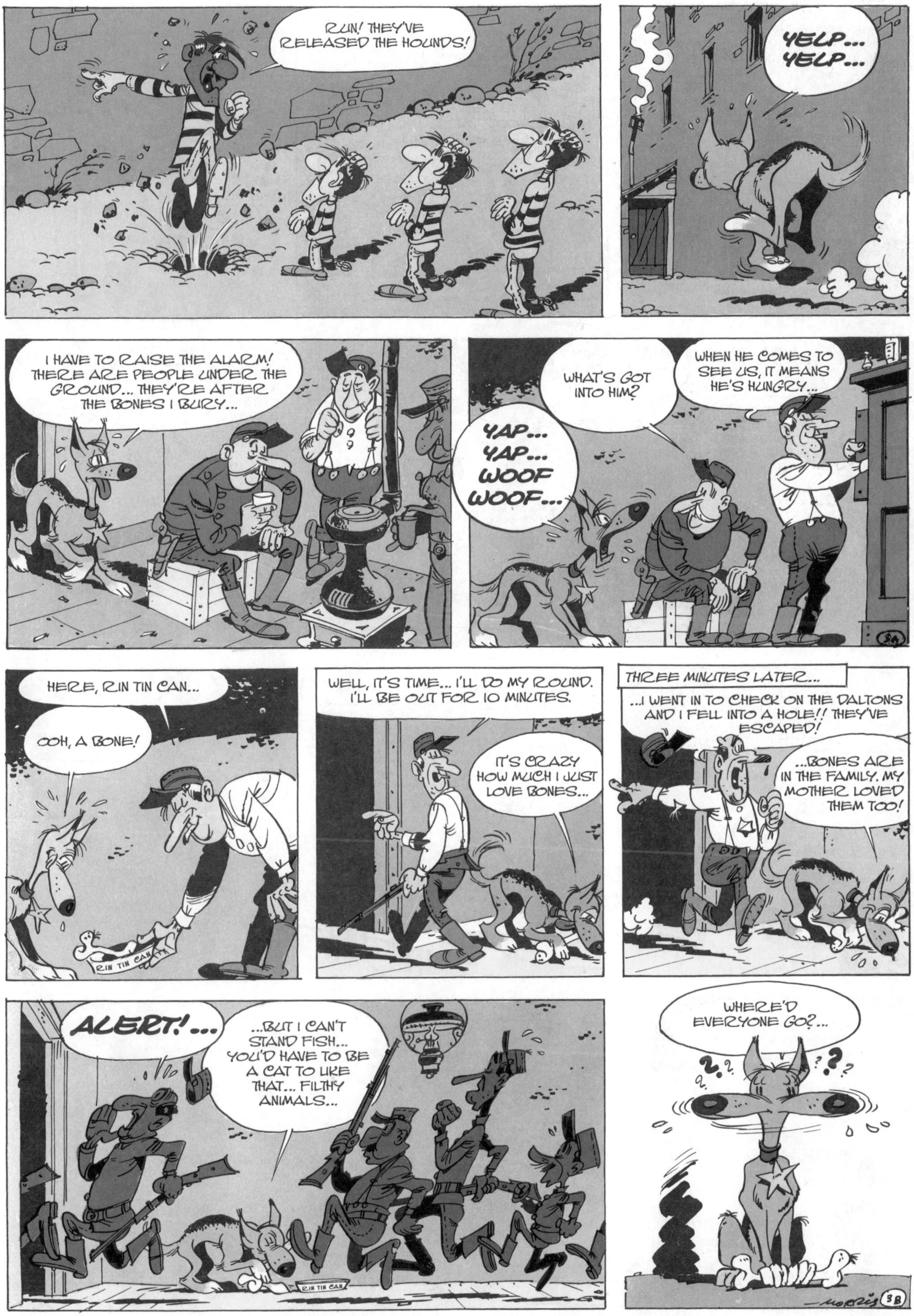
RUN! THEY'VE RELEASED THE HOUNDS!
YELP... YELP...
I HAVE TO RAISE THE ALARM! THERE ARE PEOPLE UNDER THE GROUND... THEY'RE AFTER THE BONES I BURY...
YAP... YAP... WOOF WOOF...
WHAT'S GOT INTO HIM?
WHEN HE COMES TO SEE US, IT MEANS HE'S HUNGRY...
HERE, RIN TIN CAN...
OOH, A BONE!
RIN TIN CAN
WELL, IT'S TIME... I'LL DO MY ROUND. I'LL BE OUT FOR 10 MINUTES.
IT'S CRAZY HOW MUCH I JUST LOVE BONES...
THREE MINUTES LATER...
...I WENT IN TO CHECK ON THE DALTONS AND I FELL INTO A HOLE!! THEY'VE ESCAPED!
...BONES ARE IN THE FAMILY. MY MOTHER LOVED THEM TOO!
ALERT!...
...BUT I CAN'T STAND FISH... YOU'D HAVE TO BE A CAT TO LIKE THAT... FILTHY ANIMALS...
RIN TIN CAN
WHERE'D EVERYONE GO?...
MORRIS

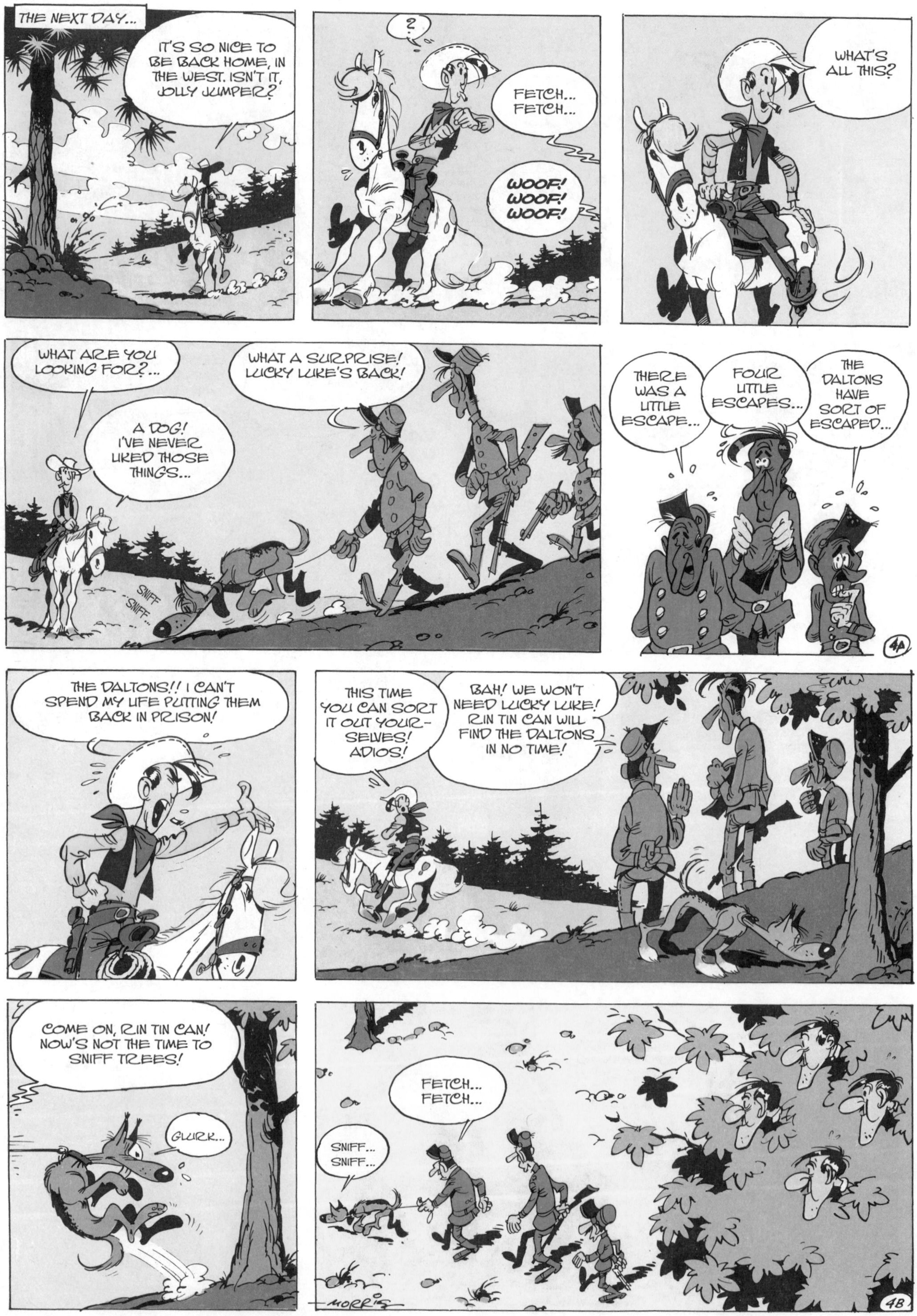
THE NEXT DAY...
IT'S SO NICE TO BE BACK HOME, IN THE WEST. ISN'T IT, JOLLY JUMPER?
?
FETCH... FETCH...
WOOF! WOOF! WOOF!
WHAT'S ALL THIS?
WHAT ARE YOU LOOKING FOR?...
A DOG! I'VE NEVER LIKED THOSE THINGS...
WHAT A SURPRISE! LUCKY LUKE'S BACK!
SNIFF SNIFF...
THERE WAS A LITTLE ESCAPE...
FOUR LITTLE ESCAPES...
THE DALTONS HAVE SORT OF ESCAPED...
4A
THE DALTONS!! I CAN'T SPEND MY LIFE PUTTING THEM BACK IN PRISON!
THIS TIME YOU CAN SORT IT OUT YOURSELVES! ADIOS!
BAH! WE WON'T NEED LUCKY LUKE! RIN TIN CAN WILL FIND THE DALTONS IN NO TIME!
COME ON, RIN TIN CAN! NOW'S NOT THE TIME TO SNIFF TREES!
GLURK...
FETCH... FETCH...
SNIFF... SNIFF...
4B

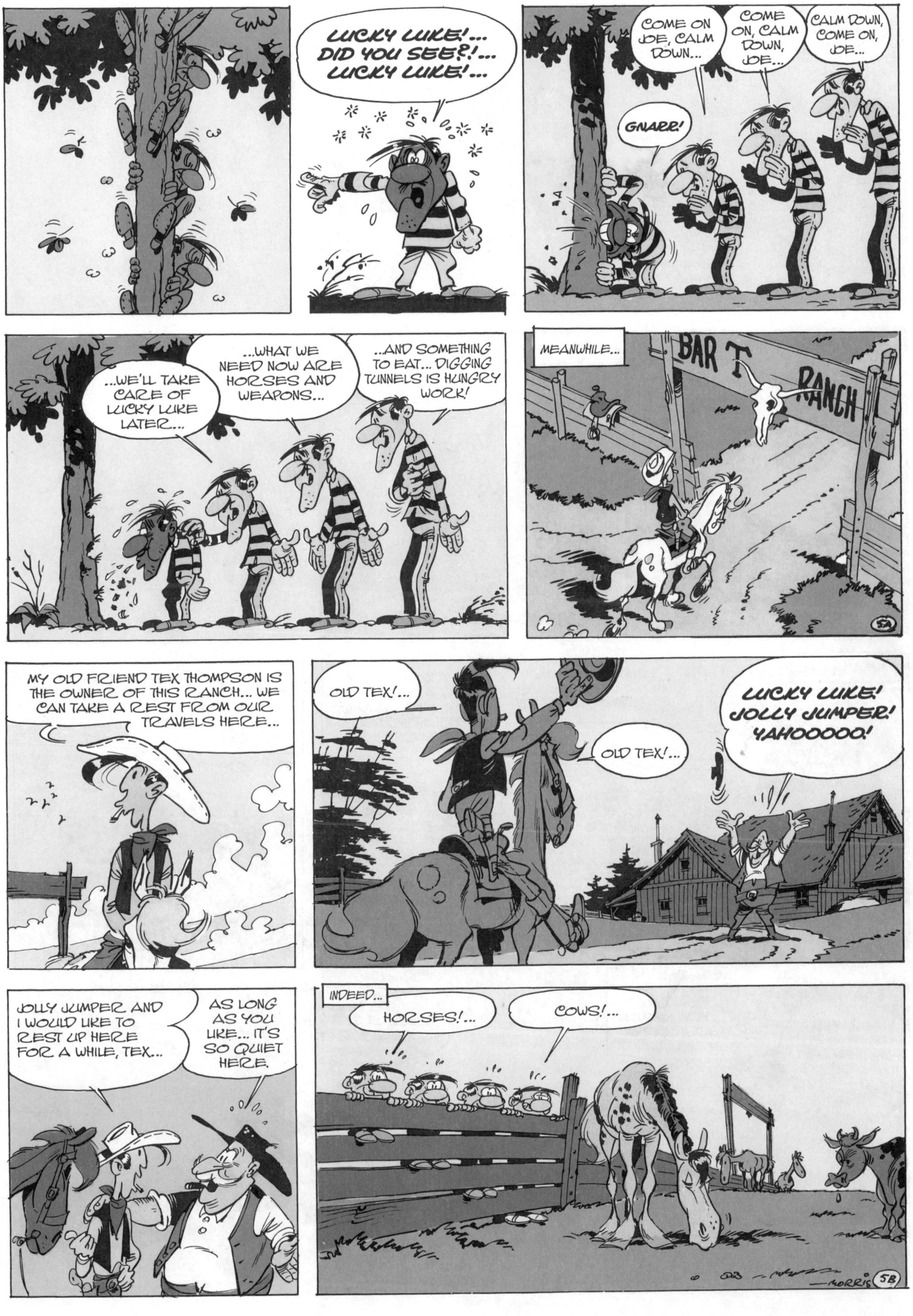
LUCKY LUKE!... DID YOU SEE?!... LUCKY LUKE!...
COME ON JOE, CALM DOWN...
COME ON, CALM DOWN, JOE...
CALM DOWN, COME ON, JOE...
GNARR!
...WE'LL TAKE CARE OF LUCKY LUKE LATER...
...WHAT WE NEED NOW ARE HORSES AND WEAPONS...
...AND SOMETHING TO EAT... DIGGING TUNNELS IS HUNGRY WORK!
MEANWHILE...
BAR T RANCH
MY OLD FRIEND TEX THOMPSON IS THE OWNER OF THIS RANCH... WE CAN TAKE A REST FROM OUR TRAVELS HERE...
OLD TEX!...
OLD TEX!...
LUCKY LUKE! JOLLY JUMPER! YAHOOOOO!
JOLLY JUMPER AND I WOULD LIKE TO REST UP HERE FOR A WHILE, TEX...
AS LONG AS YOU LIKE... IT'S SO QUIET HERE.
INDEED...
HORSES!...
COWS!...
MORRIS

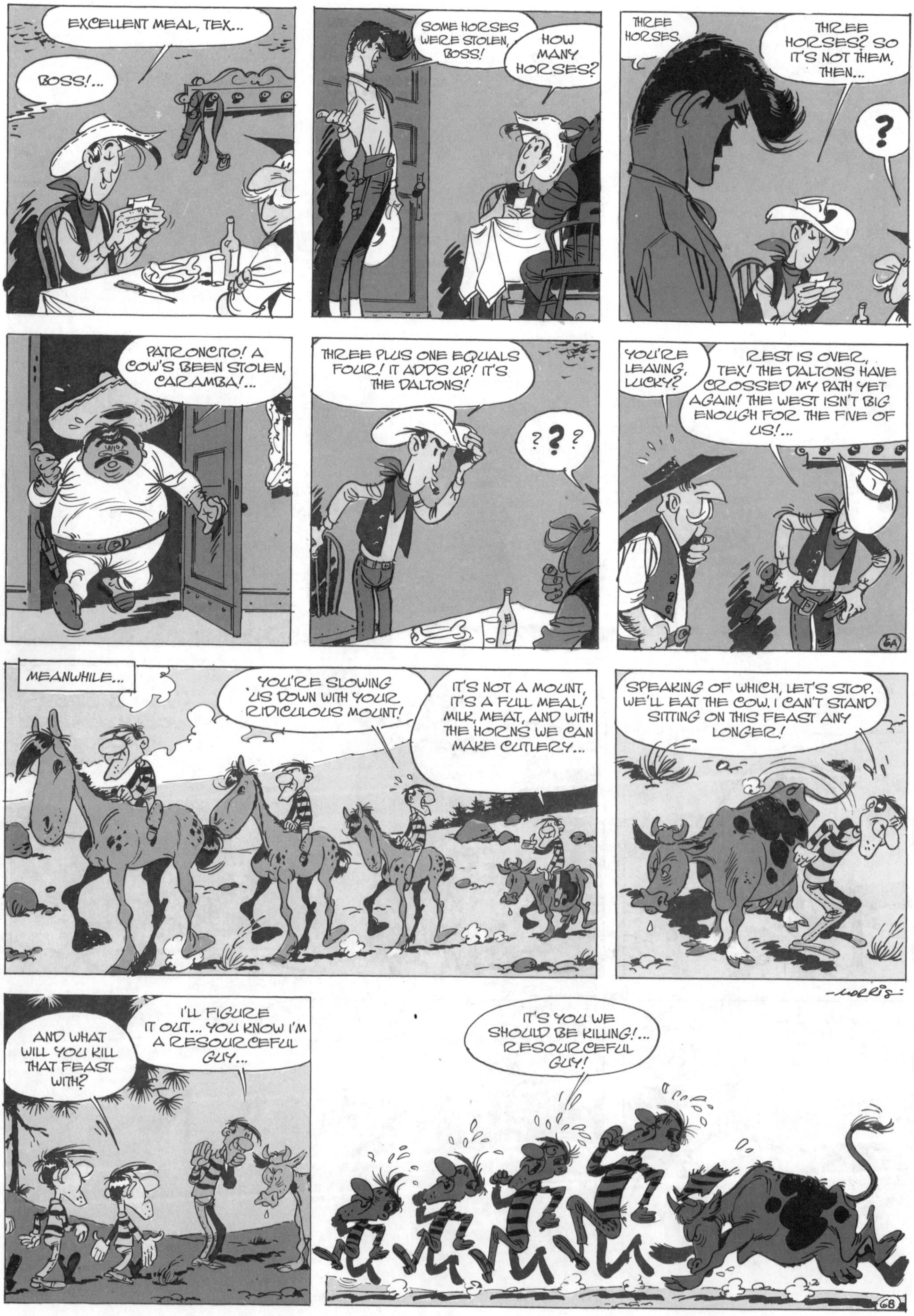

EXCELLENT MEAL, TEX...
BOSS!...
SOME HORSES WERE STOLEN, BOSS!
HOW MANY HORSES?
THREE HORSES.
THREE HORSES? SO IT'S NOT THEM, THEN...
?
PATRONCITO! A COW'S BEEN STOLEN, CARAMBA!...
THREE PLUS ONE EQUALS FOUR! IT ADDS UP! IT'S THE DALTONS!
? ? ?
YOU'RE LEAVING, LUCKY?
REST IS OVER, TEX! THE DALTONS HAVE CROSSED MY PATH YET AGAIN! THE WEST ISN'T BIG ENOUGH FOR THE FIVE OF US!...
6A
MEANWHILE...
YOU'RE SLOWING US DOWN WITH YOUR RIDICULOUS MOUNT!
IT'S NOT A MOUNT, IT'S A FULL MEAL! MILK, MEAT, AND WITH THE HORNS WE CAN MAKE CUTLERY...
SPEAKING OF WHICH, LET'S STOP. WE'LL EAT THE COW. I CAN'T STAND SITTING ON THIS FEAST ANY LONGER!
MORRIS
AND WHAT WILL YOU KILL THAT FEAST WITH?
I'LL FIGURE IT OUT... YOU KNOW I'M A RESOURCEFUL GUY...
IT'S YOU WE SHOULD BE KILLING!... RESOURCEFUL GUY!
6B

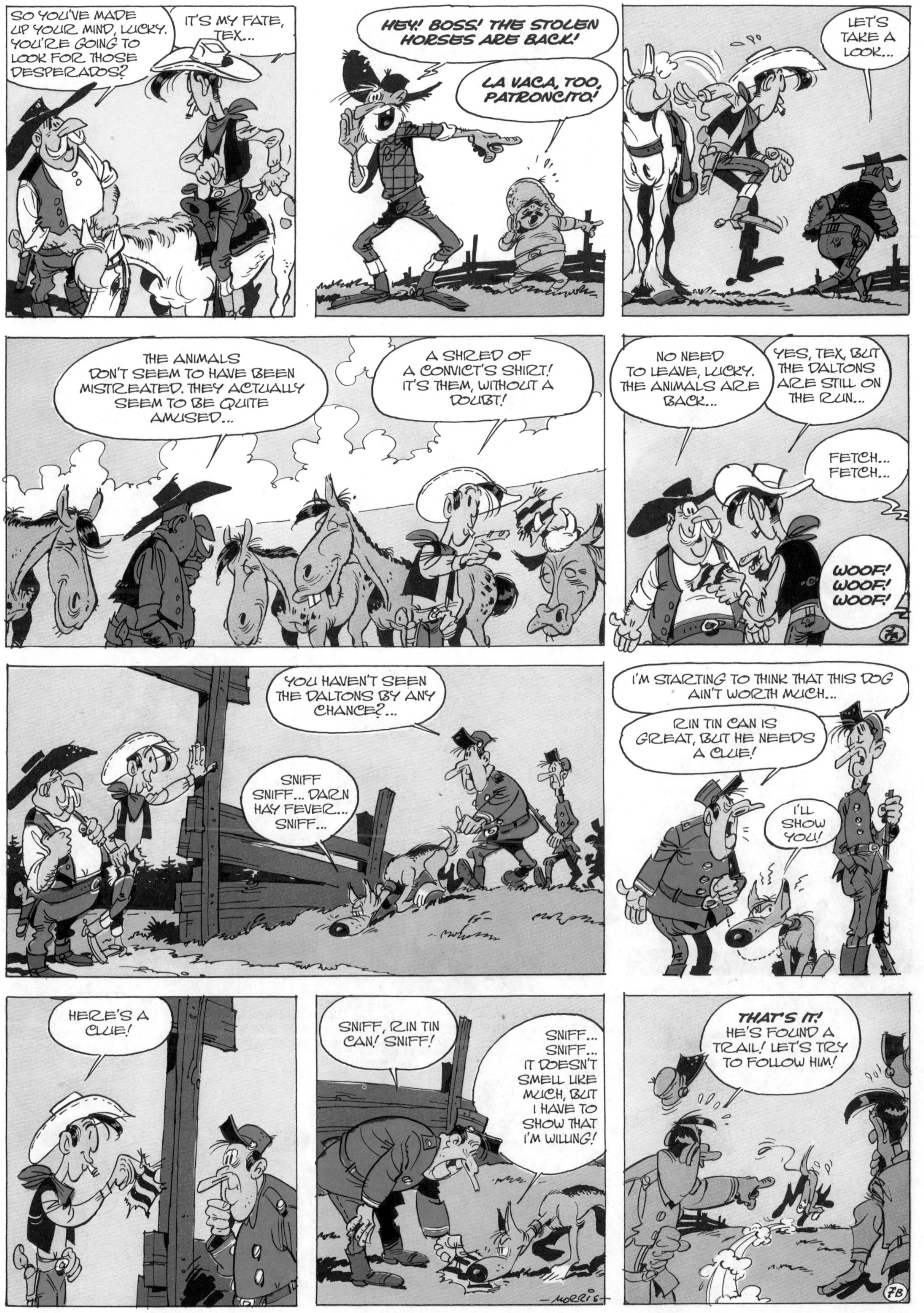
SO YOU'VE MADE UP YOUR MIND, LUCKY. YOU'RE GOING TO LOOK FOR THOSE DESPERADOS?
IT'S MY FATE, TEX...
HEY! BOSS! THE STOLEN HORSES ARE BACK!
LA VACA, TOO, PATRONCITO!
LET'S TAKE A LOOK...
THE ANIMALS DON'T SEEM TO HAVE BEEN MISTREATED. THEY ACTUALLY SEEM TO BE QUITE AMUSED...
A SHRED OF A CONVICT'S SHIRT! IT'S THEM, WITHOUT A DOUBT!
NO NEED TO LEAVE, LUCKY. THE ANIMALS ARE BACK...
YES, TEX, BUT THE DALTONS ARE STILL ON THE RUN...
FETCH... FETCH...
WOOF! WOOF! WOOF!
7A
YOU HAVEN'T SEEN THE DALTONS BY ANY CHANCE?...
SNIFF SNIFF... DARN HAY FEVER... SNIFF...
I'M STARTING TO THINK THAT THIS DOG AIN'T WORTH MUCH...
RIN TIN CAN IS GREAT, BUT HE NEEDS A CLUE!
I'LL SHOW YOU!
HERE'S A CLUE!
SNIFF, RIN TIN CAN! SNIFF!
SNIFF... SNIFF... IT DOESN'T SMELL LIKE MUCH, BUT I HAVE TO SHOW THAT I'M WILLING!
MORRIS
THAT'S IT! HE'S FOUND A TRAIL! LET'S TRY TO FOLLOW HIM!
7B

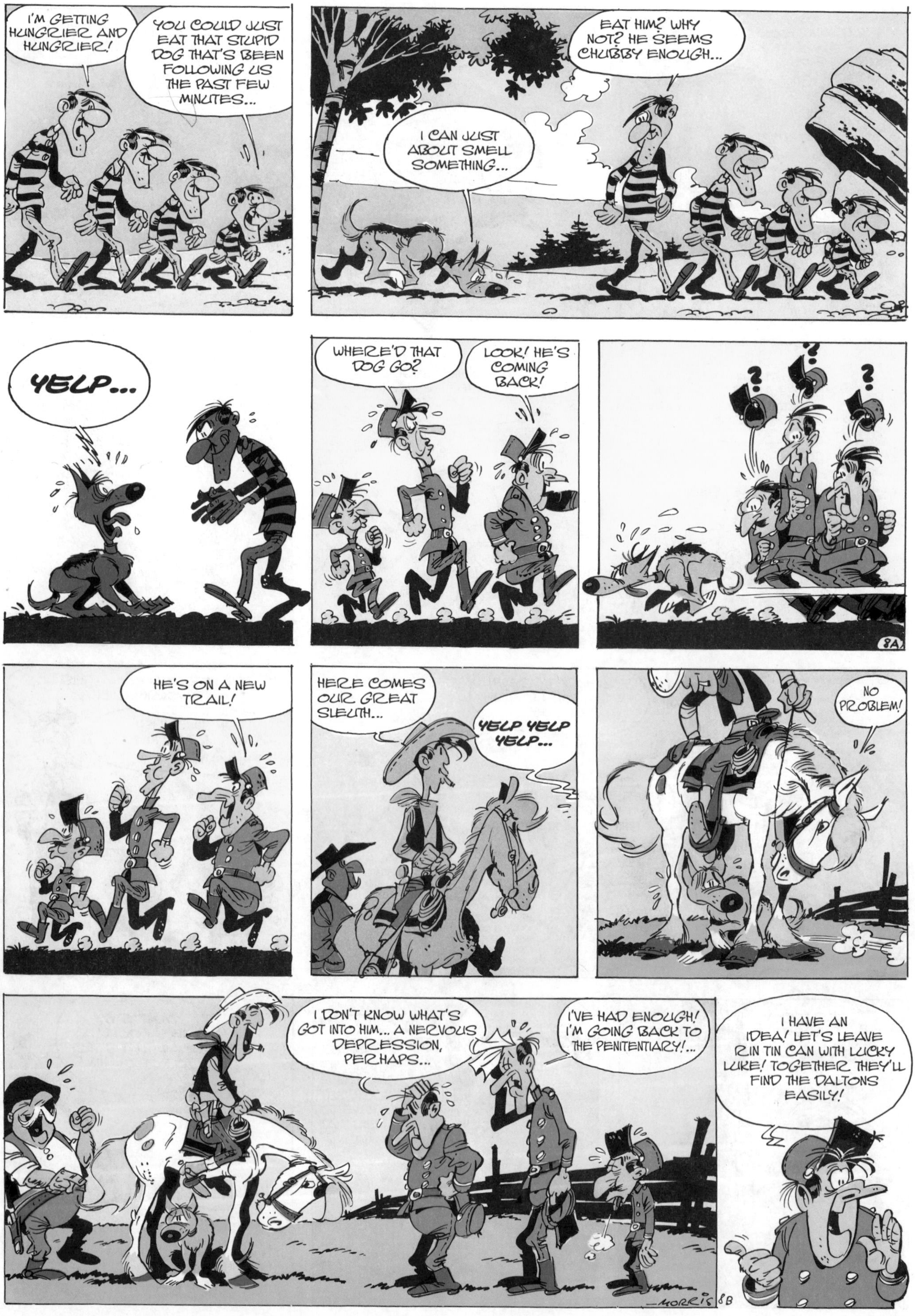
I'M GETTING HUNGRIER AND HUNGRIER!
YOU COULD JUST EAT THAT STUPID DOG THAT'S BEEN FOLLOWING US THE PAST FEW MINUTES...
EAT HIM? WHY NOT? HE SEEMS CHUBBY ENOUGH...
I CAN JUST ABOUT SMELL SOMETHING...
YELP...
WHERE'D THAT DOG GO?
LOOK! HE'S COMING BACK!
?
?
?
8A
HE'S ON A NEW TRAIL!
HERE COMES OUR GREAT SLEUTH...
YELP YELP YELP...
NO PROBLEM!
I DON'T KNOW WHAT'S GOT INTO HIM... A NERVOUS DEPRESSION, PERHAPS...
I'VE HAD ENOUGH! I'M GOING BACK TO THE PENITENTIARY!...
I HAVE AN IDEA! LET'S LEAVE RIN TIN CAN WITH LUCKY LUKE! TOGETHER THEY'LL FIND THE DALTONS EASILY!
MORRIS
8B

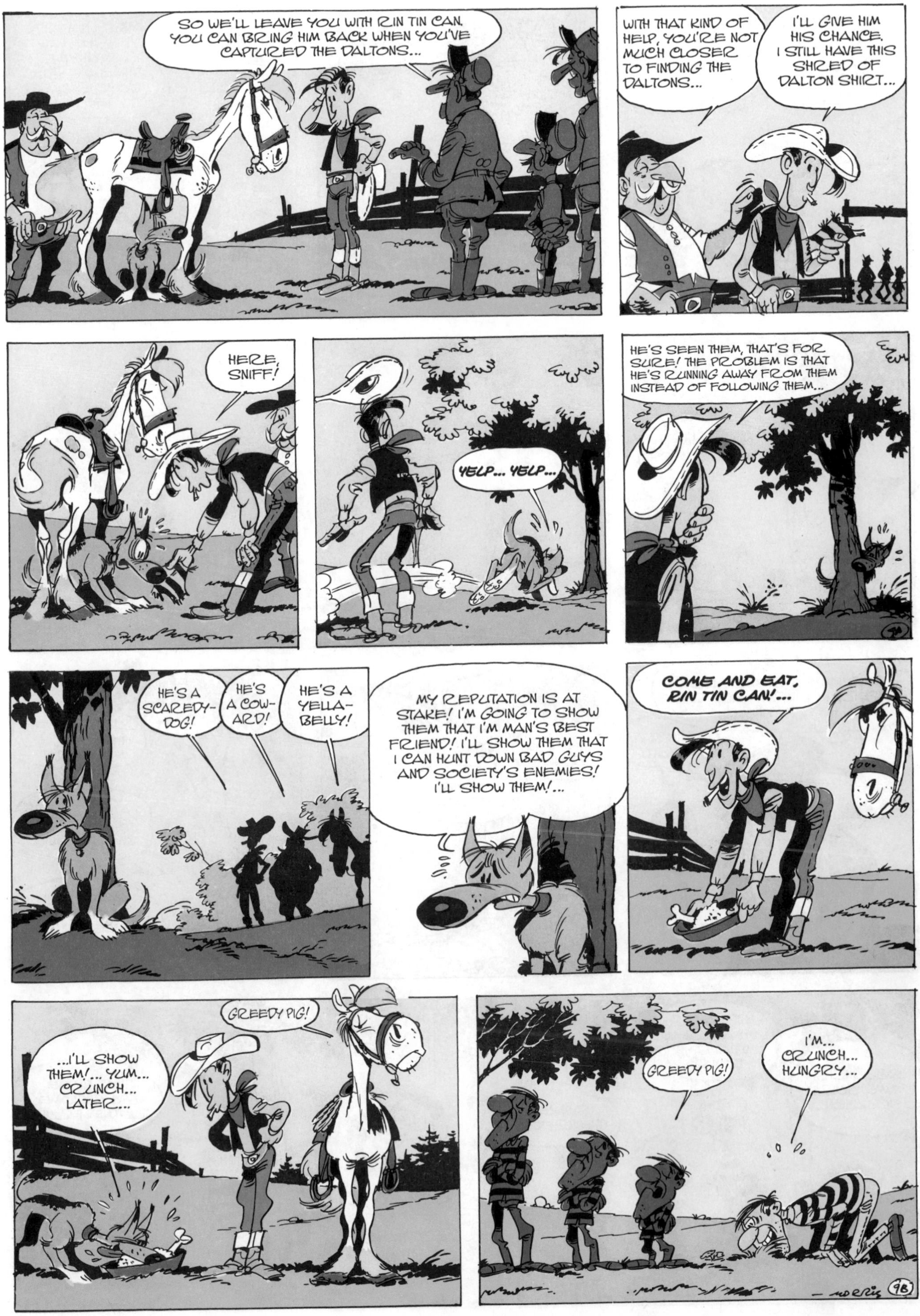

SO WE'LL LEAVE YOU WITH RIN TIN CAN. YOU CAN BRING HIM BACK WHEN YOU'VE CAPTURED THE DALTONS...
WITH THAT KIND OF HELP, YOU'RE NOT MUCH CLOSER TO FINDING THE DALTONS...
I'LL GIVE HIM HIS CHANCE. I STILL HAVE THIS SHRED OF DALTON SHIRT...
HERE, SNIFF!
YELP... YELP...
HE'S SEEN THEM, THAT'S FOR SURE! THE PROBLEM IS THAT HE'S RUNNING AWAY FROM THEM INSTEAD OF FOLLOWING THEM...
HE'S A SCAREDY-DOG!
HE'S A COW-ARD!
HE'S A YELLA-BELLY!
MY REPUTATION IS AT STAKE! I'M GOING TO SHOW THEM THAT I'M MAN'S BEST FRIEND! I'LL SHOW THEM THAT I CAN HUNT DOWN BAD GUYS AND SOCIETY'S ENEMIES! I'LL SHOW THEM!...
COME AND EAT, RIN TIN CAN!...
GREEDY PIG!
...I'LL SHOW THEM!... YUM... CRUNCH... LATER...
GREEDY PIG!
I'M... CRUNCH... HUNGRY...
MORRIS

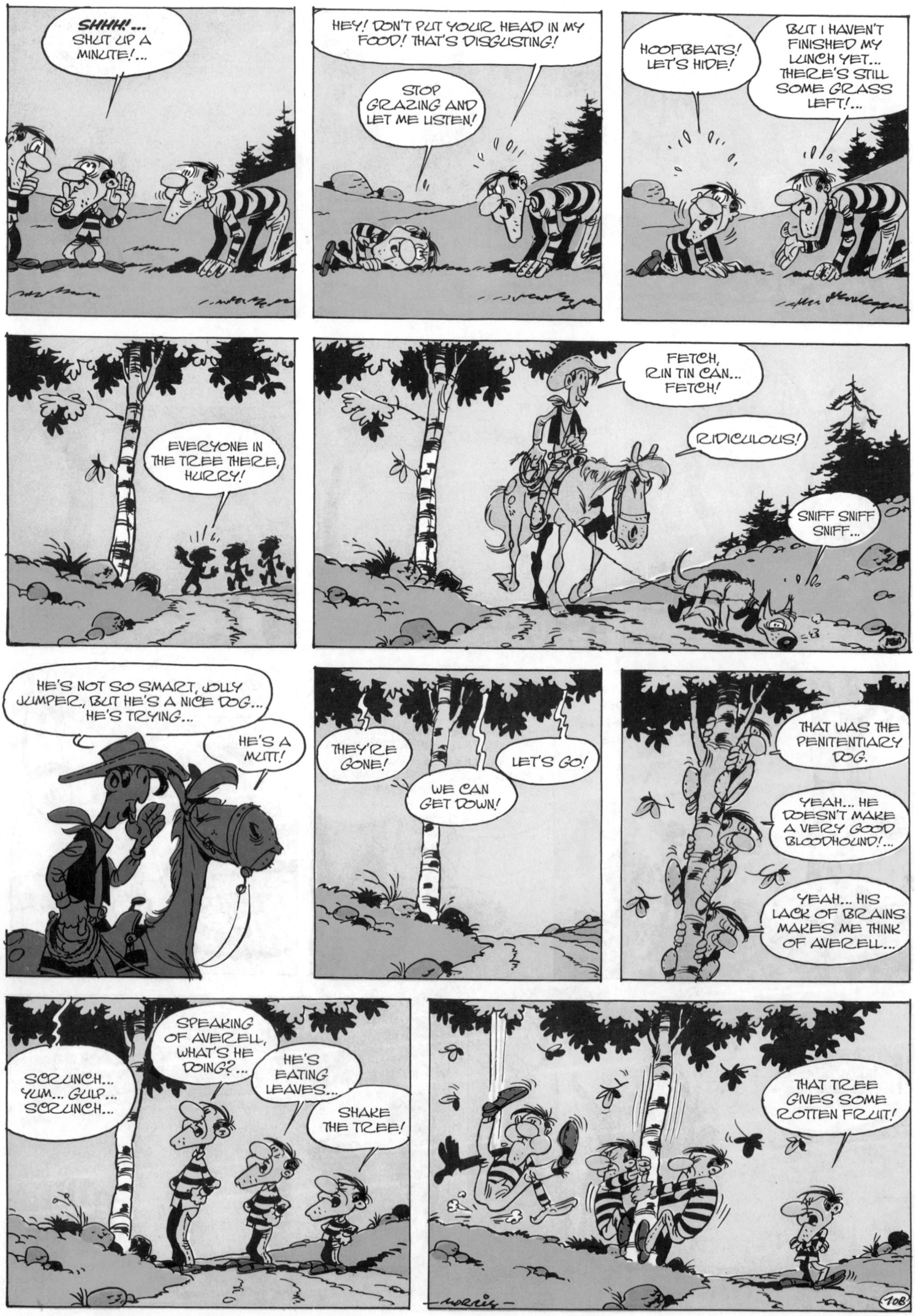
SHHH!... SHUT UP A MINUTE!...
HEY! DON'T PUT YOUR HEAD IN MY FOOD! THAT'S DISGUSTING!
STOP GRAZING AND LET ME LISTEN!
HOOFBEATS! LET'S HIDE!
BUT I HAVEN'T FINISHED MY LUNCH YET... THERE'S STILL SOME GRASS LEFT!...
EVERYONE IN THE TREE THERE, HURRY!
FETCH, RIN TIN CAN... FETCH!
RIDICULOUS!
SNIFF SNIFF SNIFF...
HE'S NOT SO SMART, JOLLY JUMPER, BUT HE'S A NICE DOG... HE'S TRYING...
HE'S A MUTT!
THEY'RE GONE!
WE CAN GET DOWN!
LET'S GO!
THAT WAS THE PENITENTIARY DOG.
YEAH... HE DOESN'T MAKE A VERY GOOD BLOODHOUND!...
YEAH... HIS LACK OF BRAINS MAKES ME THINK OF AVERELL...
SCRUNCH... YUM... GULP... SCRUNCH...
SPEAKING OF AVERELL, WHAT'S HE DOING?...
HE'S EATING LEAVES...
SHAKE THE TREE!
THAT TREE GIVES SOME ROTTEN FRUIT!

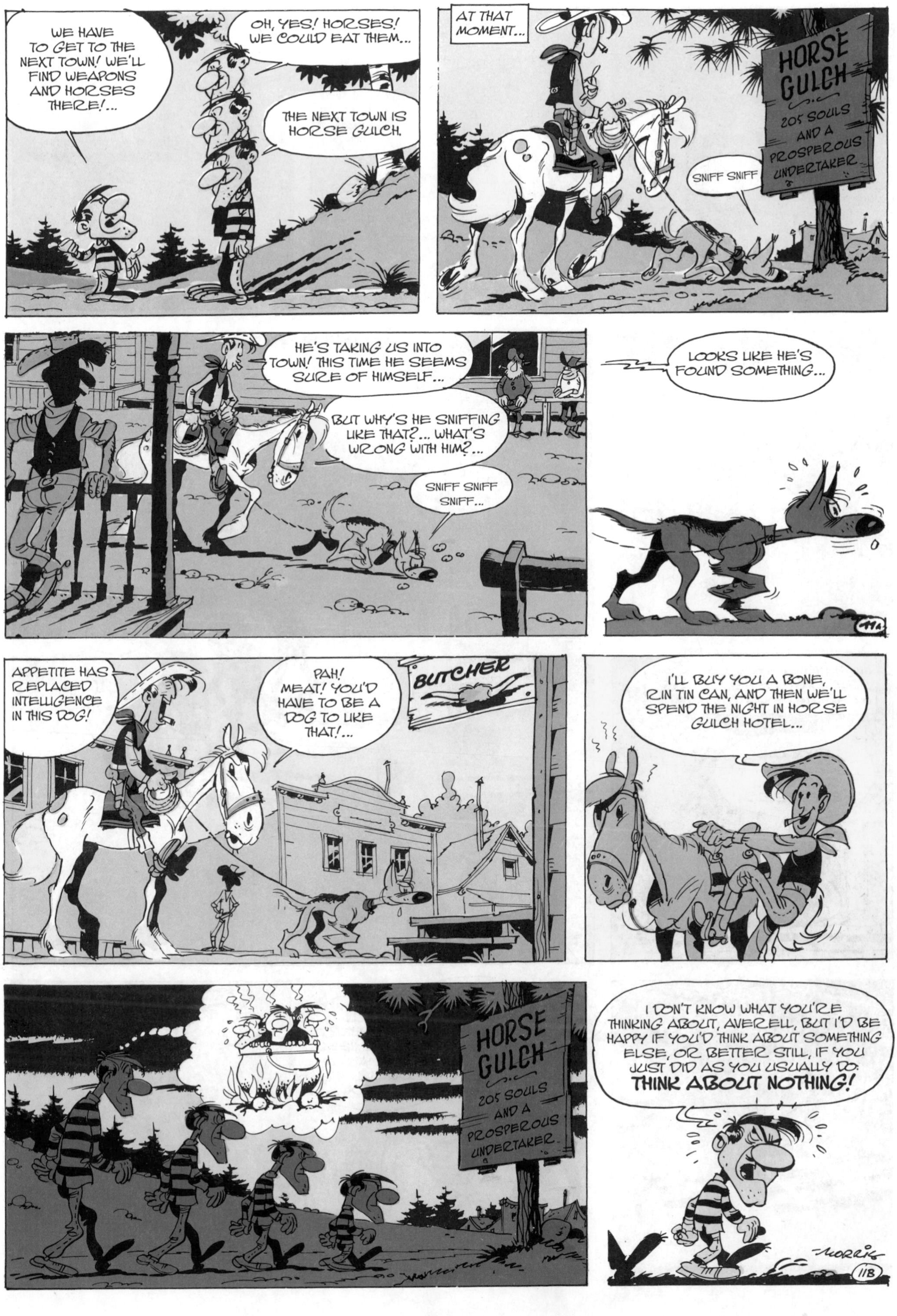
WE HAVE TO GET TO THE NEXT TOWN! WE'LL FIND WEAPONS AND HORSES THERE!...
OH, YES! HORSES! WE COULD EAT THEM...
THE NEXT TOWN IS HORSE GULCH.
AT THAT MOMENT...
HORSE GULCH
205 SOULS AND A PROSPEROUS UNDERTAKER
SNIFF SNIFF
HE'S TAKING US INTO TOWN! THIS TIME HE SEEMS SURE OF HIMSELF...
BUT WHY'S HE SNIFFING LIKE THAT?... WHAT'S WRONG WITH HIM?...
SNIFF SNIFF SNIFF...
LOOKS LIKE HE'S FOUND SOMETHING...
APPETITE HAS REPLACED INTELLIGENCE IN THIS DOG!
PAH! MEAT! YOU'D HAVE TO BE A DOG TO LIKE THAT!...
BUTCHER
I'LL BUY YOU A BONE, RIN TIN CAN, AND THEN WE'LL SPEND THE NIGHT IN HORSE GULCH HOTEL...
HORSE GULCH
205 SOULS AND A PROSPEROUS UNDERTAKER
I DON'T KNOW WHAT YOU'RE THINKING ABOUT, AVERELL, BUT I'D BE HAPPY IF YOU'D THINK ABOUT SOMETHING ELSE, OR BETTER STILL, IF YOU JUST DID AS YOU USUALLY DO: THINK ABOUT NOTHING!
MORRIS

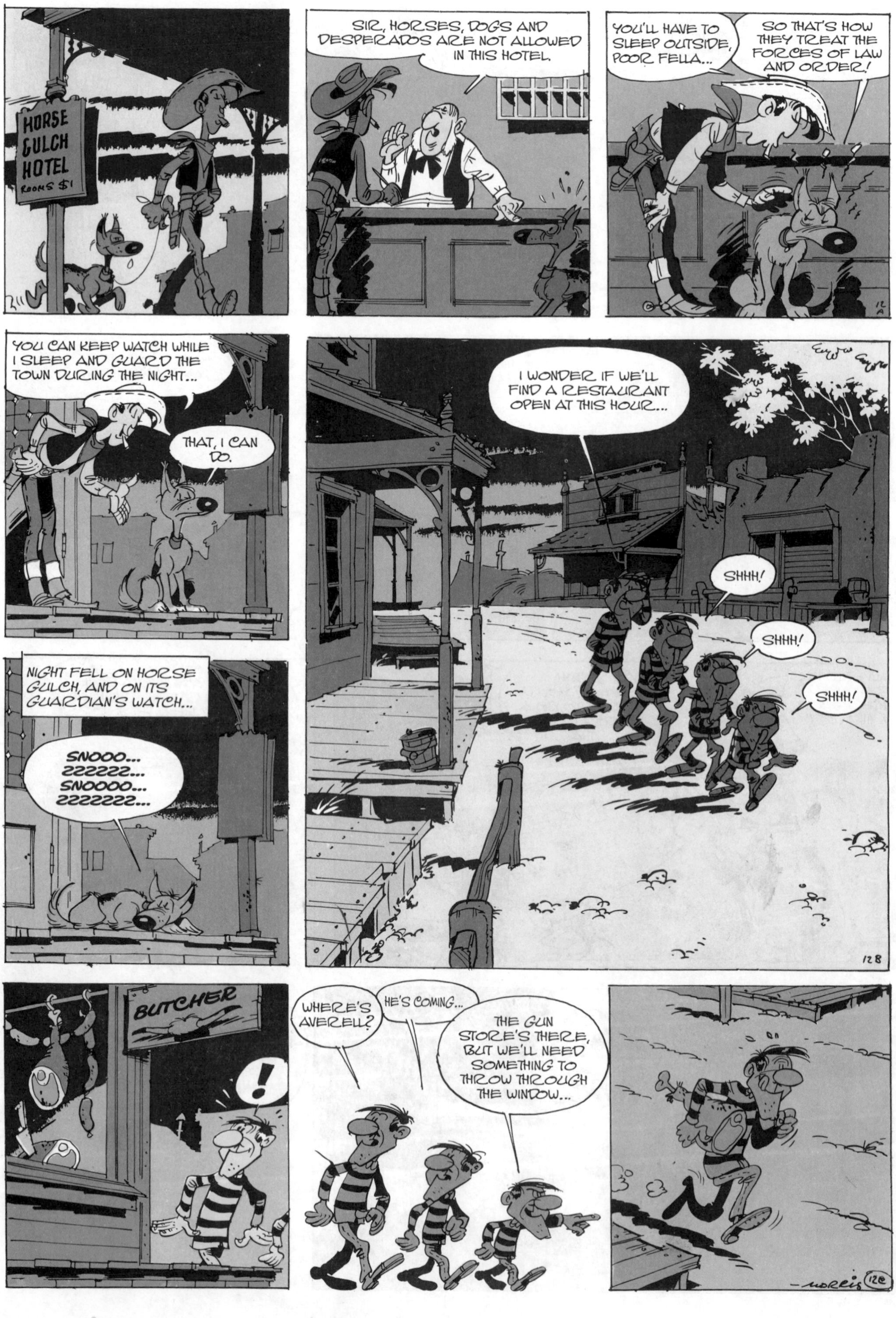
HORSE GULCH HOTEL
ROOMS $1
SIR, HORSES, DOGS AND DESPERADOS ARE NOT ALLOWED IN THIS HOTEL.
YOU'LL HAVE TO SLEEP OUTSIDE, POOR FELLA...
SO THAT'S HOW THEY TREAT THE FORCES OF LAW AND ORDER!
YOU CAN KEEP WATCH WHILE I SLEEP AND GUARD THE TOWN DURING THE NIGHT...
THAT, I CAN DO.
I WONDER IF WE'LL FIND A RESTAURANT OPEN AT THIS HOUR...
SHHH!
SHHH!
SHHH!
NIGHT FELL ON HORSE GULCH, AND ON ITS GUARDIAN'S WATCH...
SNOOO... ZZZZZZ... SNOOOO... ZZZZZZZ...
BUTCHER
!
WHERE'S AVERELL?
HE'S COMING...
THE GUN STORE'S THERE, BUT WE'LL NEED SOMETHING TO THROW THROUGH THE WINDOW...

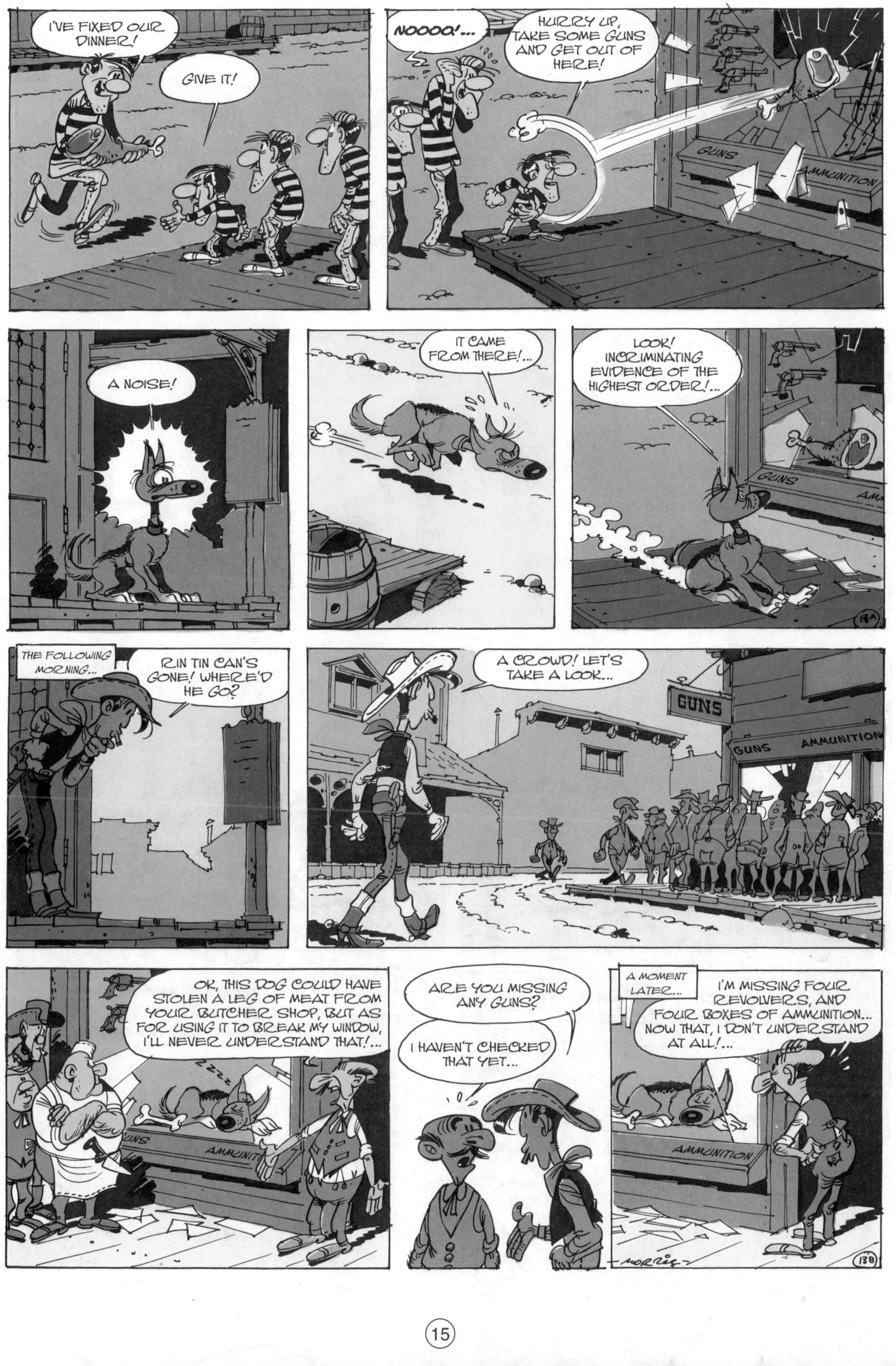
I'VE FIXED OUR DINNER!
GIVE IT!
NOOOO!...
HURRY UP, TAKE SOME GUNS AND GET OUT OF HERE!
GUNS
AMMUNITION
A NOISE!
IT CAME FROM THERE!...
LOOK! INCRIMINATING EVIDENCE OF THE HIGHEST ORDER!...
GUNS
THE FOLLOWING MORNING...
RIN TIN CAN'S GONE! WHERE'D HE GO?
A CROWD! LET'S TAKE A LOOK...
GUNS
GUNS
AMMUNITION
OK, THIS DOG COULD HAVE STOLEN A LEG OF MEAT FROM YOUR BUTCHER SHOP, BUT AS FOR USING IT TO BREAK MY WINDOW, I'LL NEVER UNDERSTAND THAT!...
ARE YOU MISSING ANY GUNS?
I HAVEN'T CHECKED THAT YET...
A MOMENT LATER...
I'M MISSING FOUR REVOLVERS, AND FOUR BOXES OF AMMUNITION... NOW THAT, I DON'T UNDERSTAND AT ALL!...
AMMUNITION
MORRIS

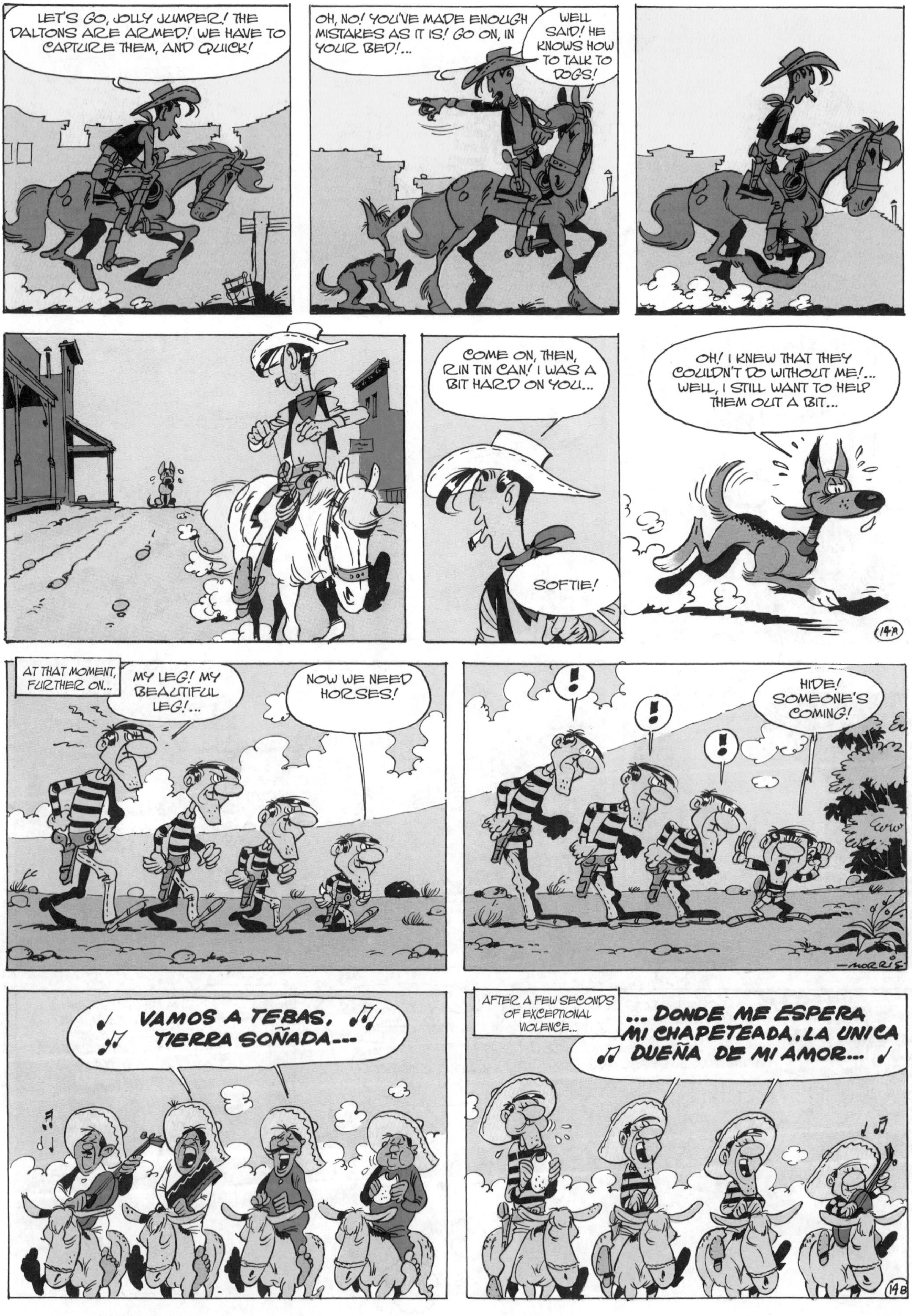
LET'S GO, JOLLY JUMPER! THE DALTONS ARE ARMED! WE HAVE TO CAPTURE THEM, AND QUICK!
OH, NO! YOU'VE MADE ENOUGH MISTAKES AS IT IS! GO ON, IN YOUR BED!...
WELL SAID! HE KNOWS HOW TO TALK TO DOGS!
COME ON, THEN, RIN TIN CAN! I WAS A BIT HARD ON YOU...
SOFTIE!
OH! I KNEW THAT THEY COULDN'T DO WITHOUT ME!... WELL, I STILL WANT TO HELP THEM OUT A BIT...
AT THAT MOMENT, FURTHER ON...
MY LEG! MY BEAUTIFUL LEG!...
NOW WE NEED HORSES!
!
!
!
HIDE! SOMEONE'S COMING!
VAMOS A TEBAS, TIERRA SOÑADA...
AFTER A FEW SECONDS OF EXCEPTIONAL VIOLENCE...
... DONDE ME ESPERA MI CHAPETEADA, LA UNICA DUEÑA DE MI AMOR...

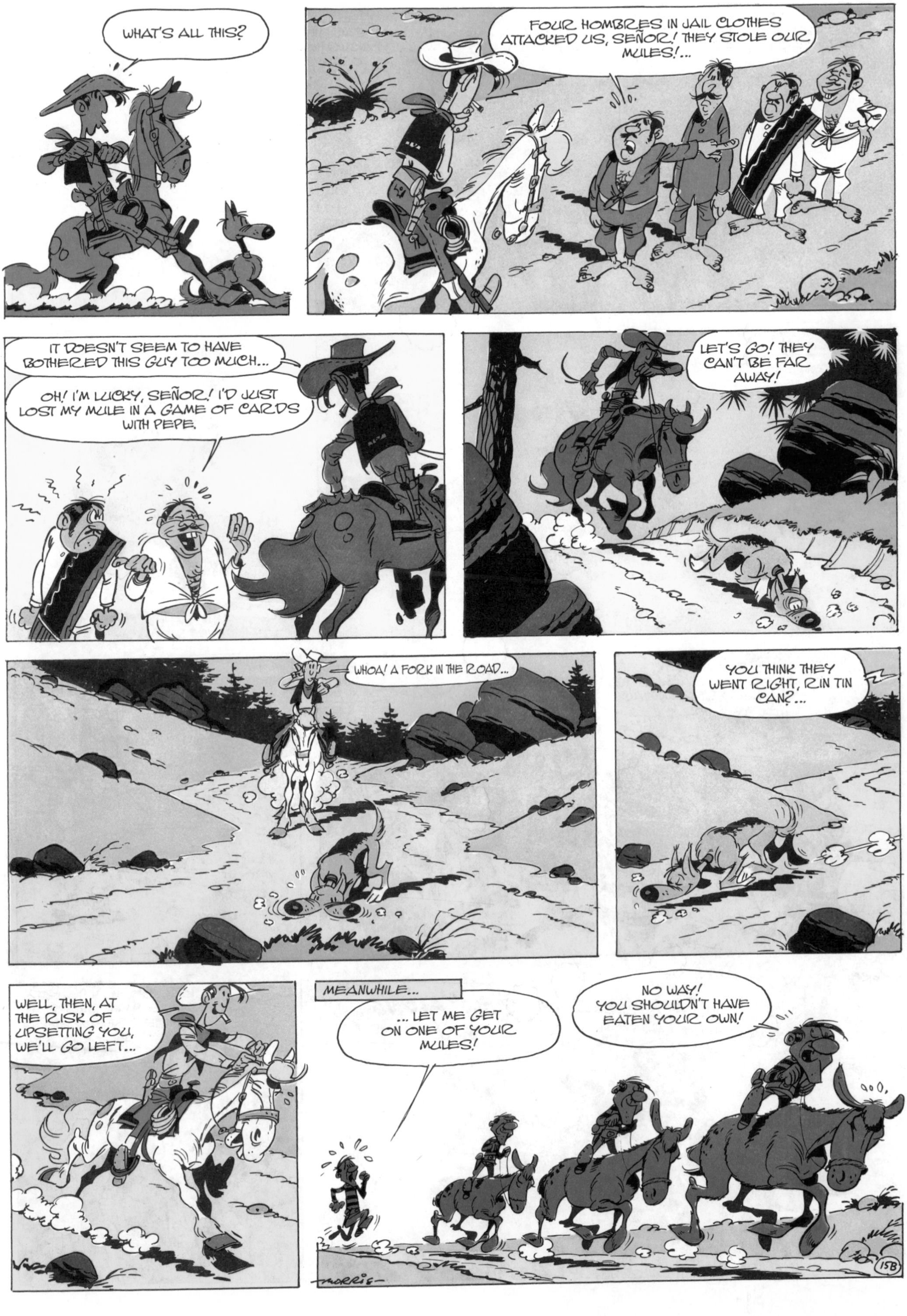
WHAT'S ALL THIS?
FOUR HOMBRES IN JAIL CLOTHES ATTACKED US, SEÑOR! THEY STOLE OUR MULES!...
IT DOESN'T SEEM TO HAVE BOTHERED THIS GUY TOO MUCH...
OH! I'M LUCKY, SEÑOR! I'D JUST LOST MY MULE IN A GAME OF CARDS WITH PEPE.
LET'S GO! THEY CAN'T BE FAR AWAY!
WHOA! A FORK IN THE ROAD...
YOU THINK THEY WENT RIGHT, RIN TIN CAN?...
WELL, THEN, AT THE RISK OF UPSETTING YOU, WE'LL GO LEFT...
MEANWHILE...
... LET ME GET ON ONE OF YOUR MULES!
NO WAY! YOU SHOULDN'T HAVE EATEN YOUR OWN!
15B
MORRIS

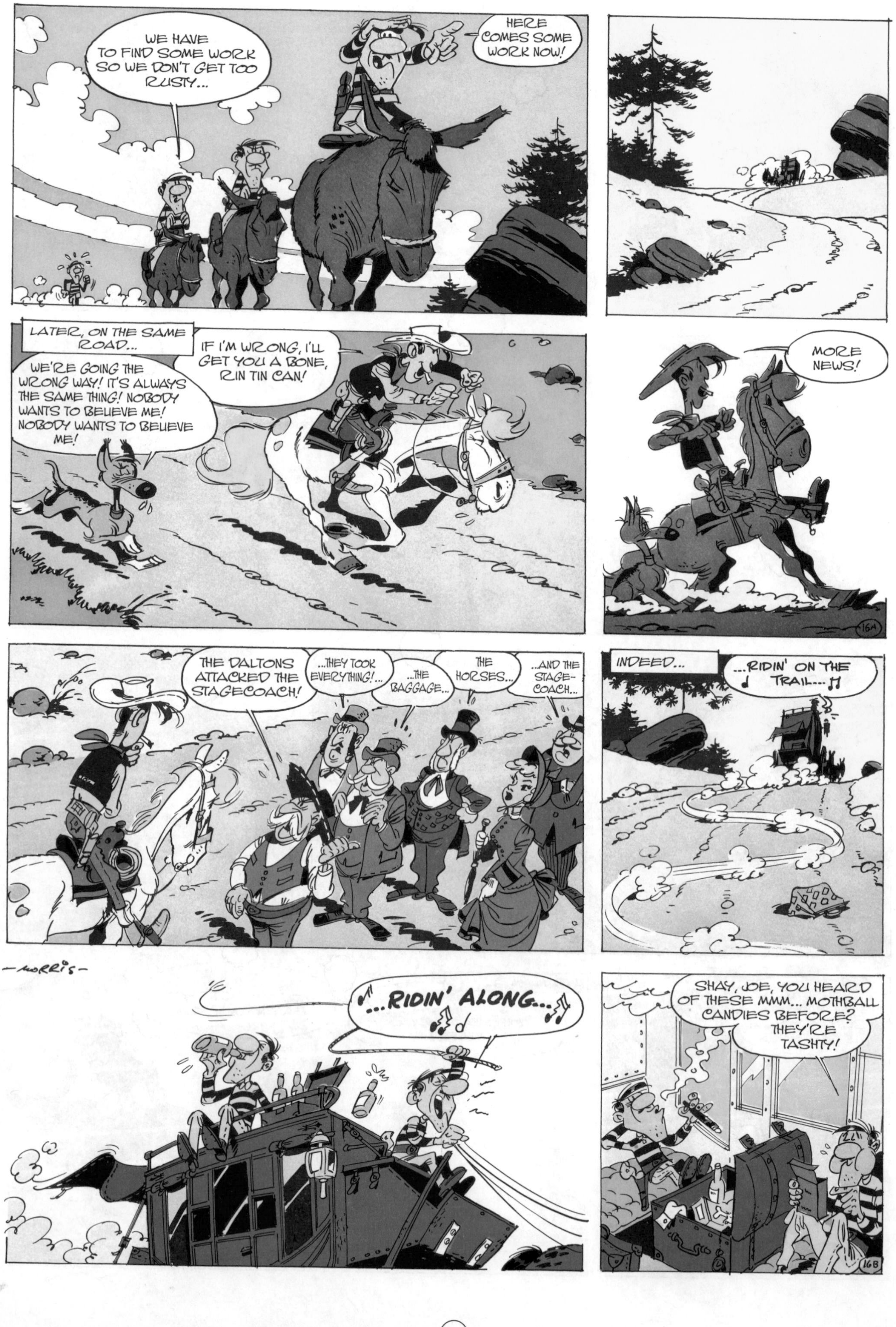
WE HAVE TO FIND SOME WORK SO WE DON'T GET TOO RUSTY...
HERE COMES SOME WORK NOW!
LATER, ON THE SAME ROAD...
WE'RE GOING THE WRONG WAY! IT'S ALWAYS THE SAME THING! NOBODY WANTS TO BELIEVE ME! NOBODY WANTS TO BELIEVE ME!
IF I'M WRONG, I'LL GET YOU A BONE, RIN TIN CAN!
MORE NEWS!
THE DALTONS ATTACKED THE STAGECOACH!
...THEY TOOK EVERYTHING!...
...THE BAGGAGE...
THE HORSES...
...AND THE STAGE-COACH...
INDEED...
...RIDIN' ON THE TRAIL...
MORRIS
...RIDIN' ALONG...
SHAY, JOE, YOU HEARD OF THESE MMM... MOTHBALL CANDIES BEFORE? THEY'RE TASHTY!

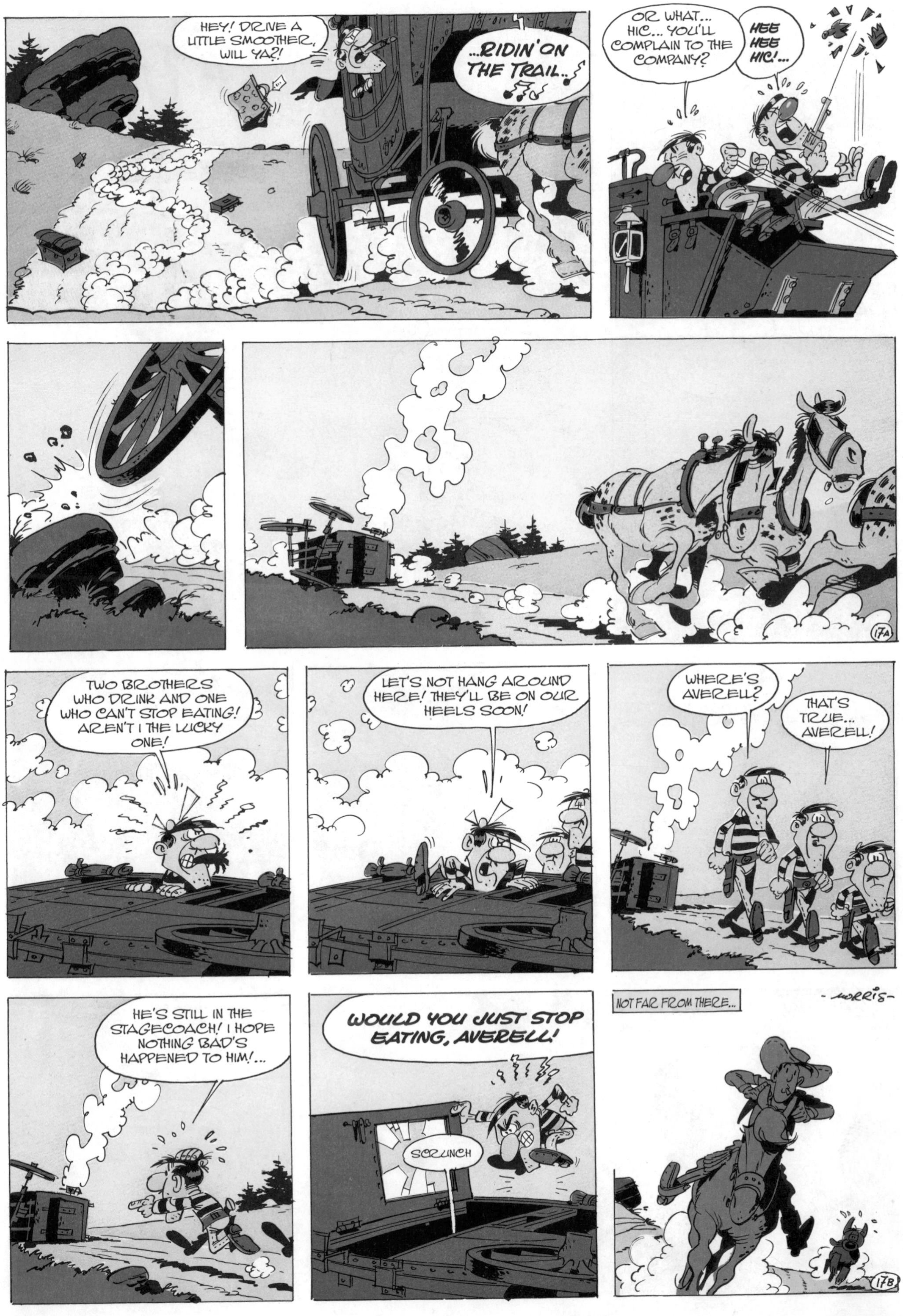
HEY! DRIVE A LITTLE SMOOTHER, WILL YA?!
...RIDIN' ON THE TRAIL...
OR WHAT... HIC... YOU'LL COMPLAIN TO THE COMPANY?
HEE HEE HIC!...
TWO BROTHERS WHO DRINK AND ONE WHO CAN'T STOP EATING! AREN'T I THE LUCKY ONE!
LET'S NOT HANG AROUND HERE! THEY'LL BE ON OUR HEELS SOON!
WHERE'S AVERELL?
THAT'S TRUE... AVERELL!
HE'S STILL IN THE STAGECOACH! I HOPE NOTHING BAD'S HAPPENED TO HIM!...
WOULD YOU JUST STOP EATING, AVERELL!
SCRUNCH
NOT FAR FROM THERE...
-MORRIS-

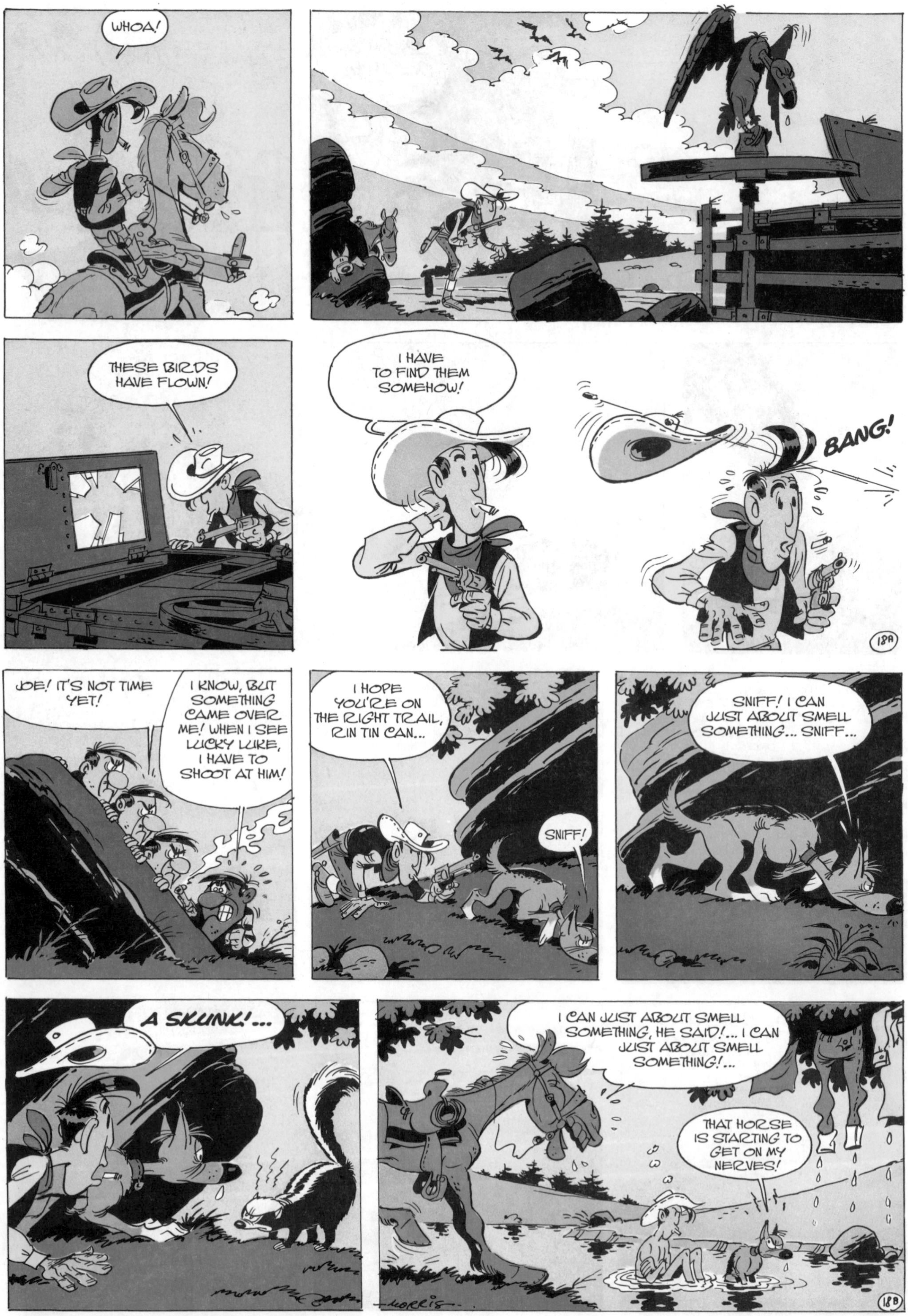
WHOA!
THESE BIRDS HAVE FLOWN!
I HAVE TO FIND THEM SOMEHOW!
BANG!
18A
JOE! IT'S NOT TIME YET!
I KNOW, BUT SOMETHING CAME OVER ME! WHEN I SEE LUCKY LUKE, I HAVE TO SHOOT AT HIM!
I HOPE YOU'RE ON THE RIGHT TRAIL, RIN TIN CAN...
SNIFF!
SNIFF! I CAN JUST ABOUT SMELL SOMETHING... SNIFF...
A SKUNK!...
I CAN JUST ABOUT SMELL SOMETHING, HE SAID!... I CAN JUST ABOUT SMELL SOMETHING!...
THAT HORSE IS STARTING TO GET ON MY NERVES!
MORRIS
18B

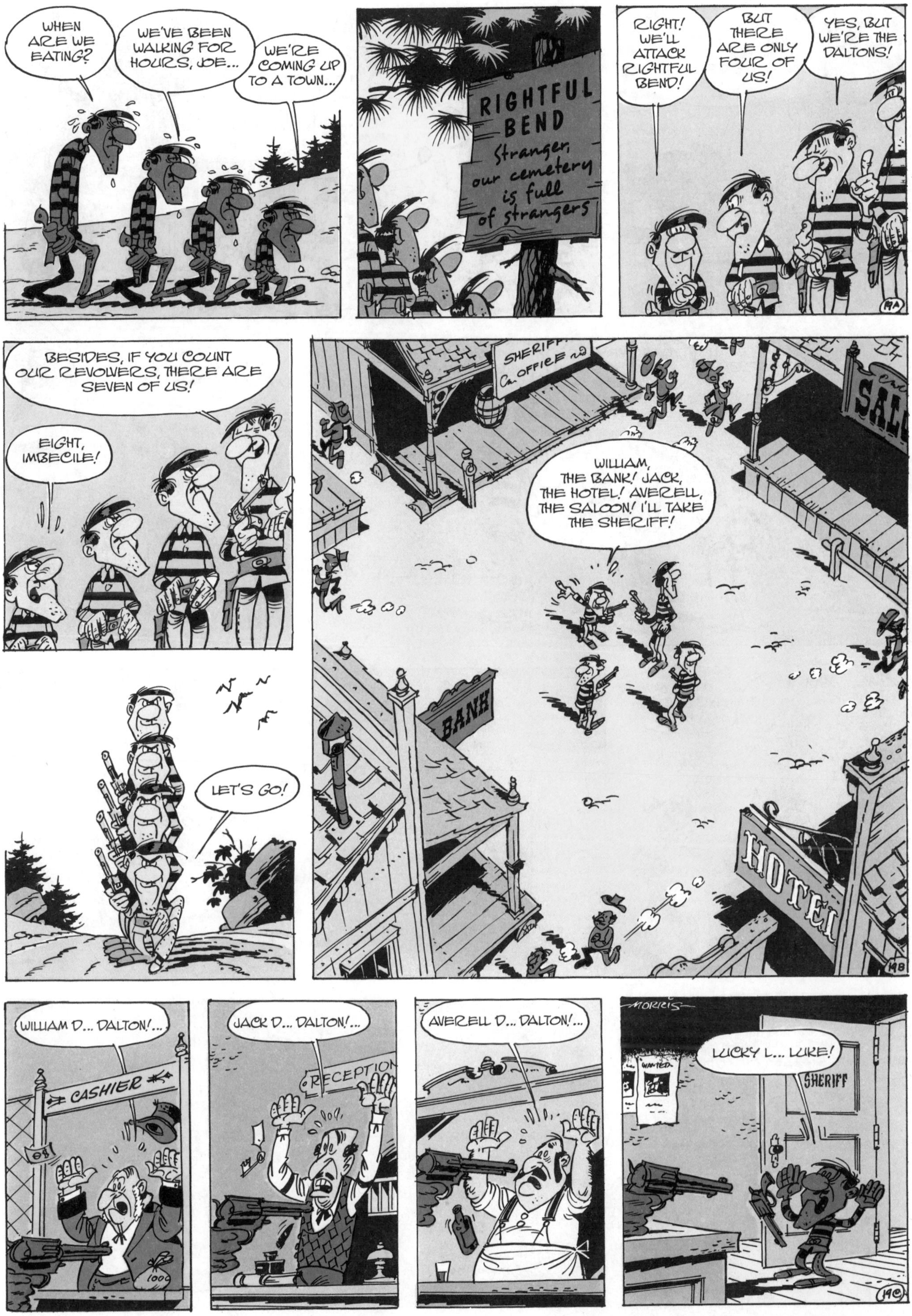
WHEN ARE WE EATING?
WE'VE BEEN WALKING FOR HOURS, JOE...
WE'RE COMING UP TO A TOWN...
RIGHTFUL BEND
Stranger, our cemetery is full of strangers
RIGHT! WE'LL ATTACK RIGHTFUL BEND!
BUT THERE ARE ONLY FOUR OF US!
YES, BUT WE'RE THE DALTONS!
BESIDES, IF YOU COUNT OUR REVOLVERS, THERE ARE SEVEN OF US!
EIGHT, IMBECILE!
SHERIFF OFFICE
WILLIAM, THE BANK! JACK, THE HOTEL! AVERELL, THE SALOON! I'LL TAKE THE SHERIFF!
BANK
HOTEL
LET'S GO!
WILLIAM D... DALTON!...
CASHIER
JACK D... DALTON!...
RECEPTION
AVERELL D... DALTON!...
MORRIS
WANTED
LUCKY L... LUKE!
SHERIFF

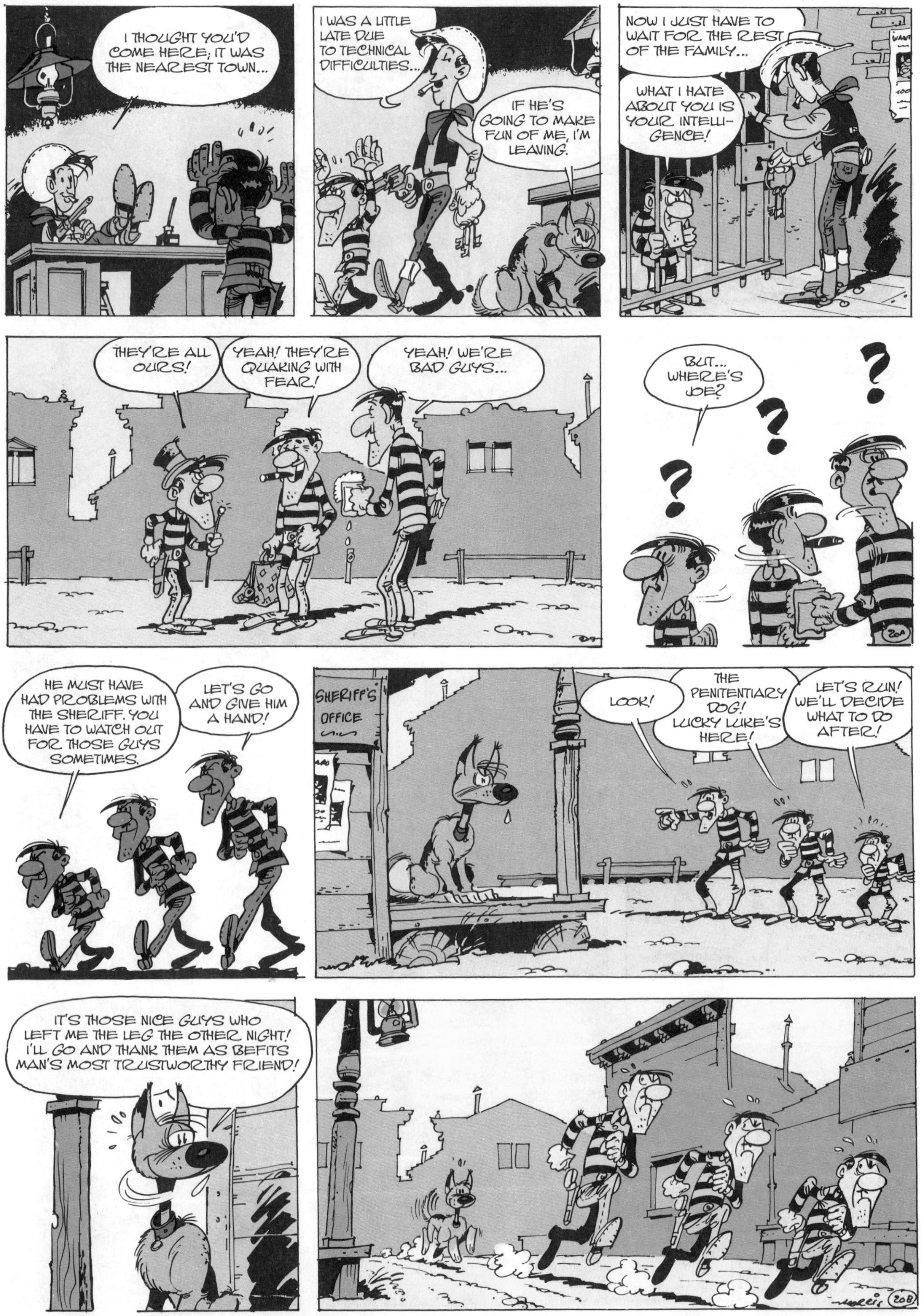
I THOUGHT YOU'D COME HERE; IT WAS THE NEAREST TOWN...
I WAS A LITTLE LATE DUE TO TECHNICAL DIFFICULTIES...
IF HE'S GOING TO MAKE FUN OF ME, I'M LEAVING.
NOW I JUST HAVE TO WAIT FOR THE REST OF THE FAMILY...
WHAT I HATE ABOUT YOU IS YOUR INTELLI-GENCE!
THEY'RE ALL OURS!
YEAH! THEY'RE QUAKING WITH FEAR!
YEAH! WE'RE BAD GUYS...
BUT... WHERE'S JOE?
HE MUST HAVE HAD PROBLEMS WITH THE SHERIFF. YOU HAVE TO WATCH OUT FOR THOSE GUYS SOMETIMES.
LET'S GO AND GIVE HIM A HAND!
SHERIFF'S OFFICE
LOOK!
THE PENITENTIARY DOG! LUCKY LUKE'S HERE!
LET'S RUN! WE'LL DECIDE WHAT TO DO AFTER!
IT'S THOSE NICE GUYS WHO LEFT ME THE LEG THE OTHER NIGHT! I'LL GO AND THANK THEM AS BEFITS MAN'S MOST TRUSTWORTHY FRIEND!

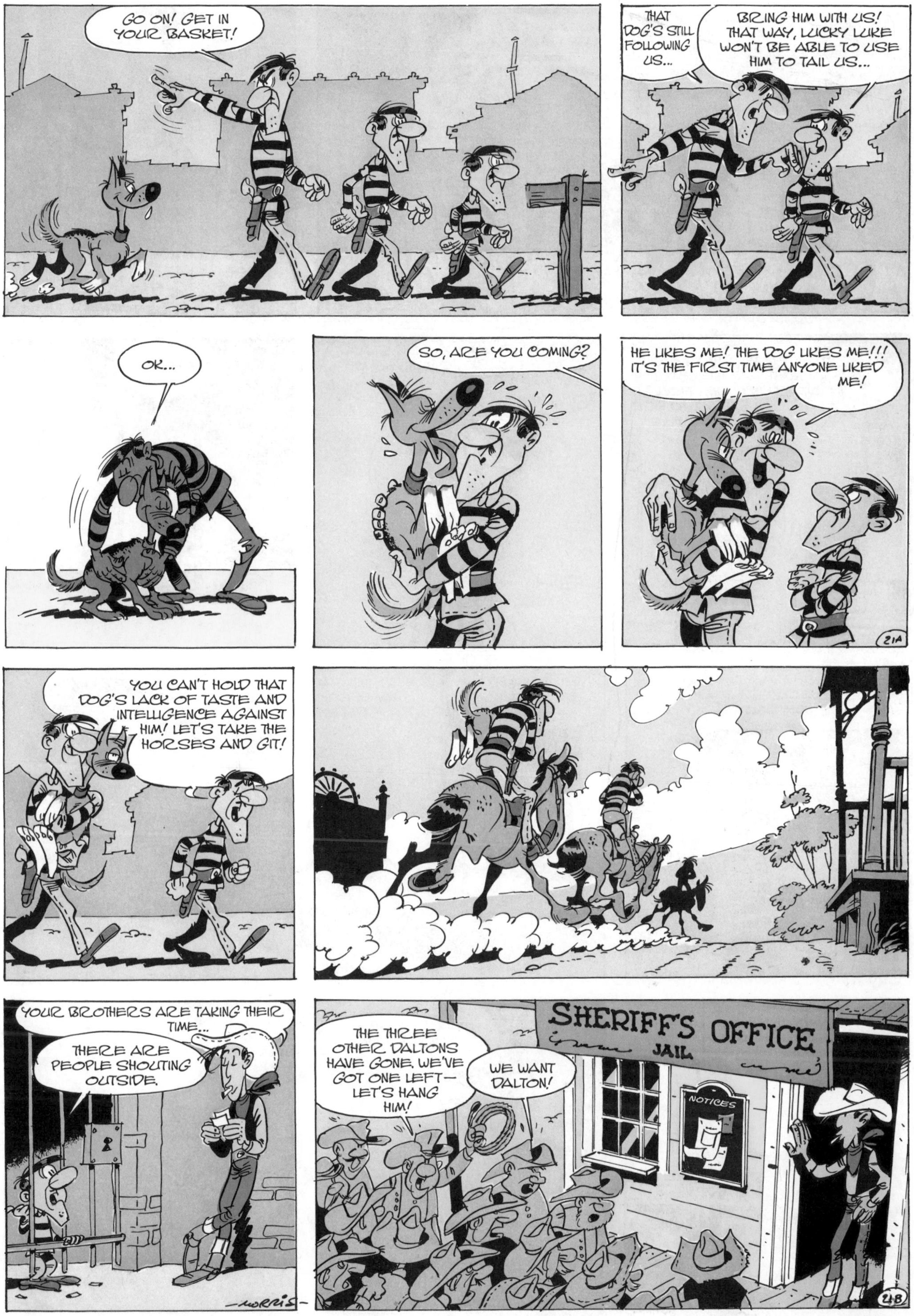

GO ON! GET IN YOUR BASKET!
THAT DOG'S STILL FOLLOWING US...
BRING HIM WITH US! THAT WAY, LUCKY LUKE WON'T BE ABLE TO USE HIM TO TAIL US...
OK...
SO, ARE YOU COMING?
HE LIKES ME! THE DOG LIKES ME!!! IT'S THE FIRST TIME ANYONE LIKED ME!
YOU CAN'T HOLD THAT DOG'S LACK OF TASTE AND INTELLIGENCE AGAINST HIM! LET'S TAKE THE HORSES AND GIT!
YOUR BROTHERS ARE TAKING THEIR TIME...
THERE ARE PEOPLE SHOUTING OUTSIDE.
SHERIFF'S OFFICE
JAIL
NOTICES
THE THREE OTHER DALTONS HAVE GONE. WE'VE GOT ONE LEFT— LET'S HANG HIM!
WE WANT DALTON!

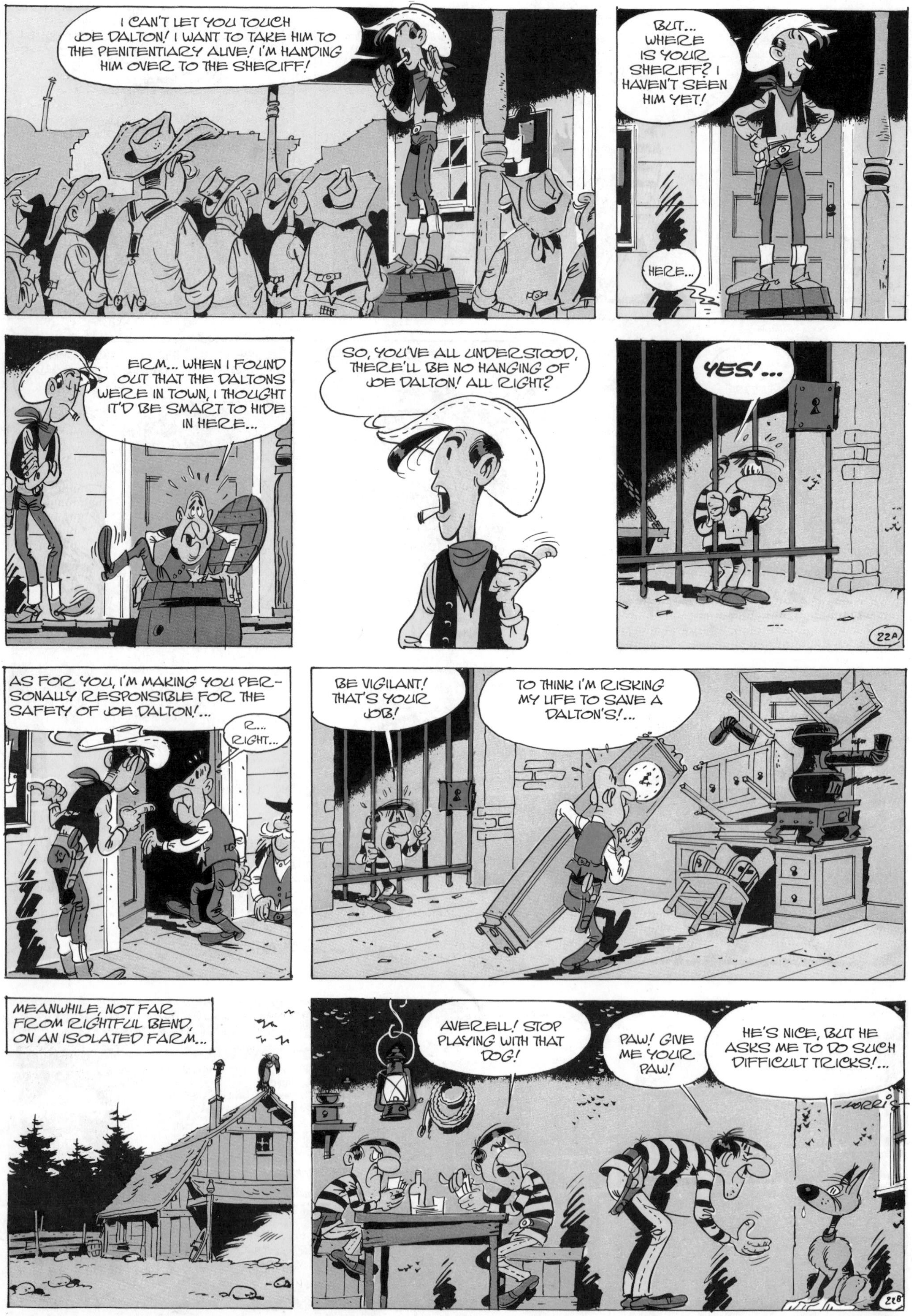

I CAN'T LET YOU TOUCH JOE DALTON! I WANT TO TAKE HIM TO THE PENITENTIARY ALIVE! I'M HANDING HIM OVER TO THE SHERIFF!
BUT... WHERE IS YOUR SHERIFF? I HAVEN'T SEEN HIM YET!
HERE...
ERM... WHEN I FOUND OUT THAT THE DALTONS WERE IN TOWN, I THOUGHT IT'D BE SMART TO HIDE IN HERE...
SO, YOU'VE ALL UNDERSTOOD, THERE'LL BE NO HANGING OF JOE DALTON! ALL RIGHT?
YES!...
22A
AS FOR YOU, I'M MAKING YOU PERSONALLY RESPONSIBLE FOR THE SAFETY OF JOE DALTON!...
R... RIGHT...
BE VIGILANT! THAT'S YOUR JOB!
TO THINK I'M RISKING MY LIFE TO SAVE A DALTON'S!...
MEANWHILE, NOT FAR FROM RIGHTFUL BEND, ON AN ISOLATED FARM...
AVERELL! STOP PLAYING WITH THAT DOG!
PAW! GIVE ME YOUR PAW!
HE'S NICE, BUT HE ASKS ME TO DO SUCH DIFFICULT TRICKS!...
MORRIS
22B

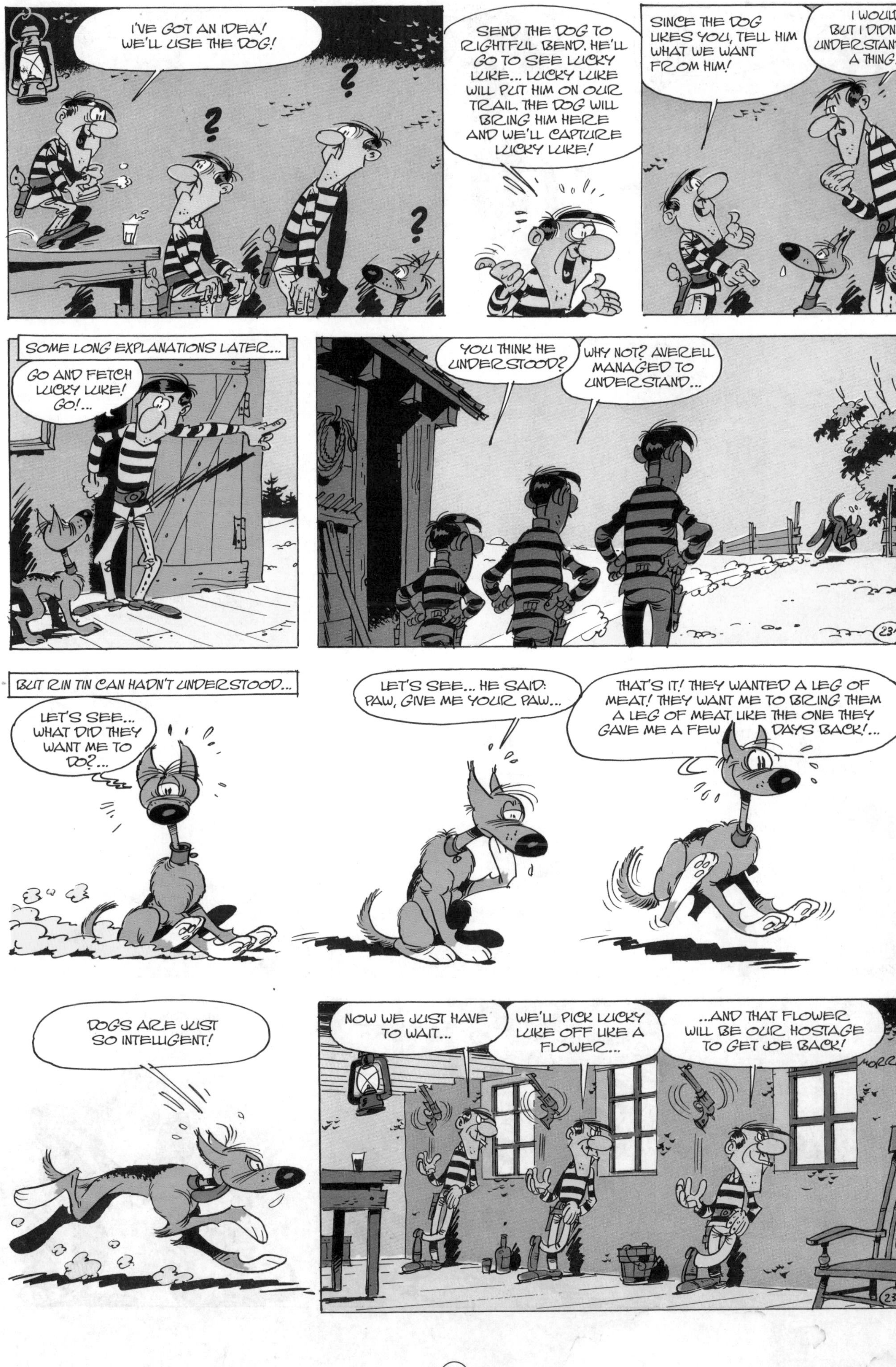
I'VE GOT AN IDEA! WE'LL USE THE DOG!
?
?
?
SEND THE DOG TO RIGHTFUL BEND. HE'LL GO TO SEE LUCKY LUKE... LUCKY LUKE WILL PUT HIM ON OUR TRAIL. THE DOG WILL BRING HIM HERE AND WE'LL CAPTURE LUCKY LUKE!
SINCE THE DOG LIKES YOU, TELL HIM WHAT WE WANT FROM HIM!
I WOULD, BUT I DIDN'T UNDERSTAND A THING...
SOME LONG EXPLANATIONS LATER...
GO AND FETCH LUCKY LUKE! GO!...
YOU THINK HE UNDERSTOOD?
WHY NOT? AVERELL MANAGED TO UNDERSTAND...
23A
BUT RIN TIN CAN HADN'T UNDERSTOOD...
LET'S SEE... WHAT DID THEY WANT ME TO DO?...
LET'S SEE... HE SAID: PAW, GIVE ME YOUR PAW...
THAT'S IT! THEY WANTED A LEG OF MEAT! THEY WANT ME TO BRING THEM A LEG OF MEAT LIKE THE ONE THEY GAVE ME A FEW DAYS BACK!...
DOGS ARE JUST SO INTELLIGENT!
NOW WE JUST HAVE TO WAIT...
WE'LL PICK LUCKY LUKE OFF LIKE A FLOWER...
...AND THAT FLOWER WILL BE OUR HOSTAGE TO GET JOE BACK!
MORRIS
23B

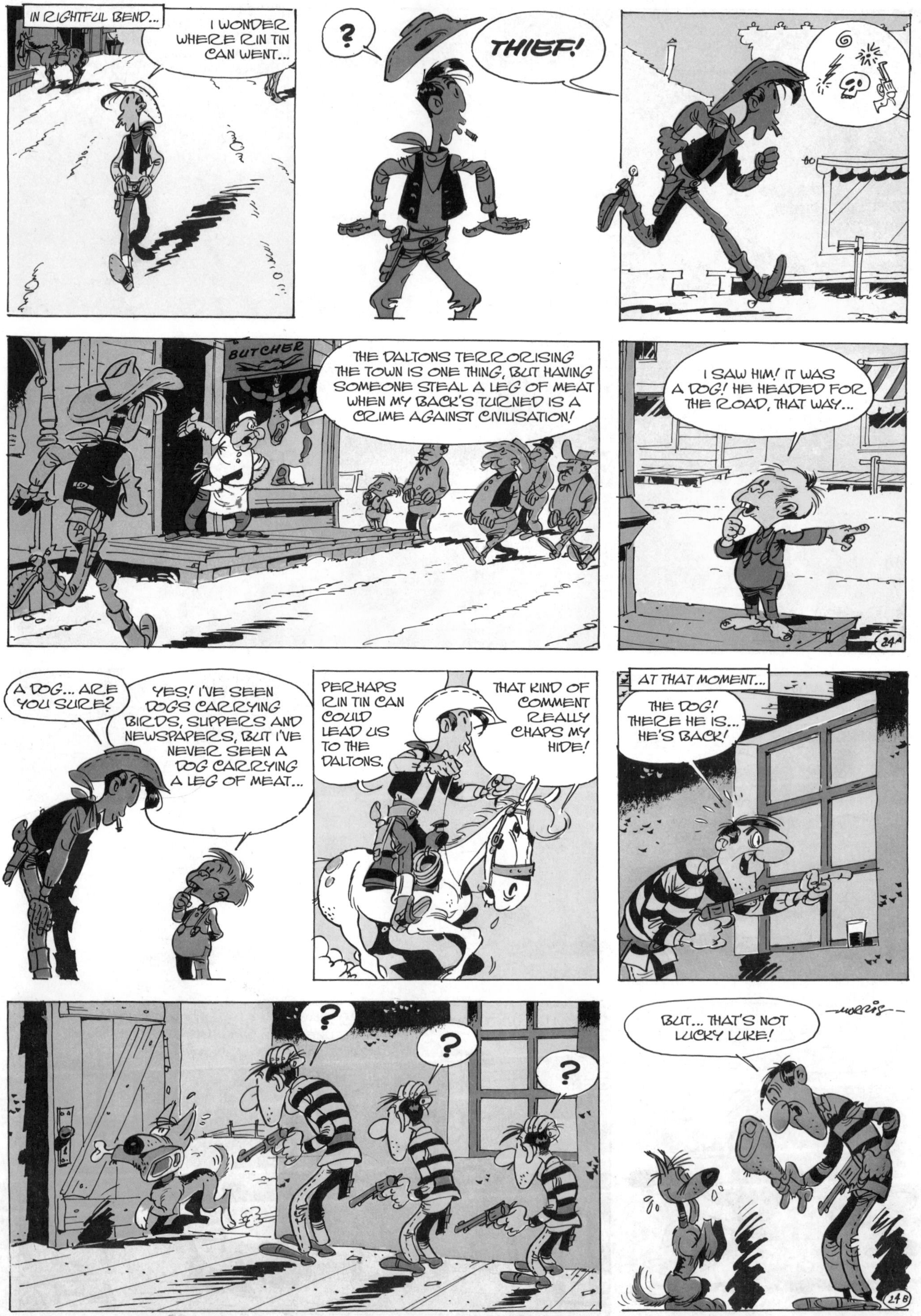

IN RIGHTFUL BEND...
I WONDER WHERE RIN TIN CAN WENT...
?
THIEF!
BUTCHER
THE DALTONS TERRORISING THE TOWN IS ONE THING, BUT HAVING SOMEONE STEAL A LEG OF MEAT WHEN MY BACK'S TURNED IS A CRIME AGAINST CIVILISATION!
I SAW HIM! IT WAS A DOG! HE HEADED FOR THE ROAD, THAT WAY...
A DOG... ARE YOU SURE?
YES! I'VE SEEN DOGS CARRYING BIRDS, SLIPPERS AND NEWSPAPERS, BUT I'VE NEVER SEEN A DOG CARRYING A LEG OF MEAT...
PERHAPS RIN TIN CAN COULD LEAD US TO THE DALTONS.
THAT KIND OF COMMENT REALLY CHAPS MY HIDE!
AT THAT MOMENT...
THE DOG! THERE HE IS... HE'S BACK!
?
?
?
BUT... THAT'S NOT LUCKY LUKE!

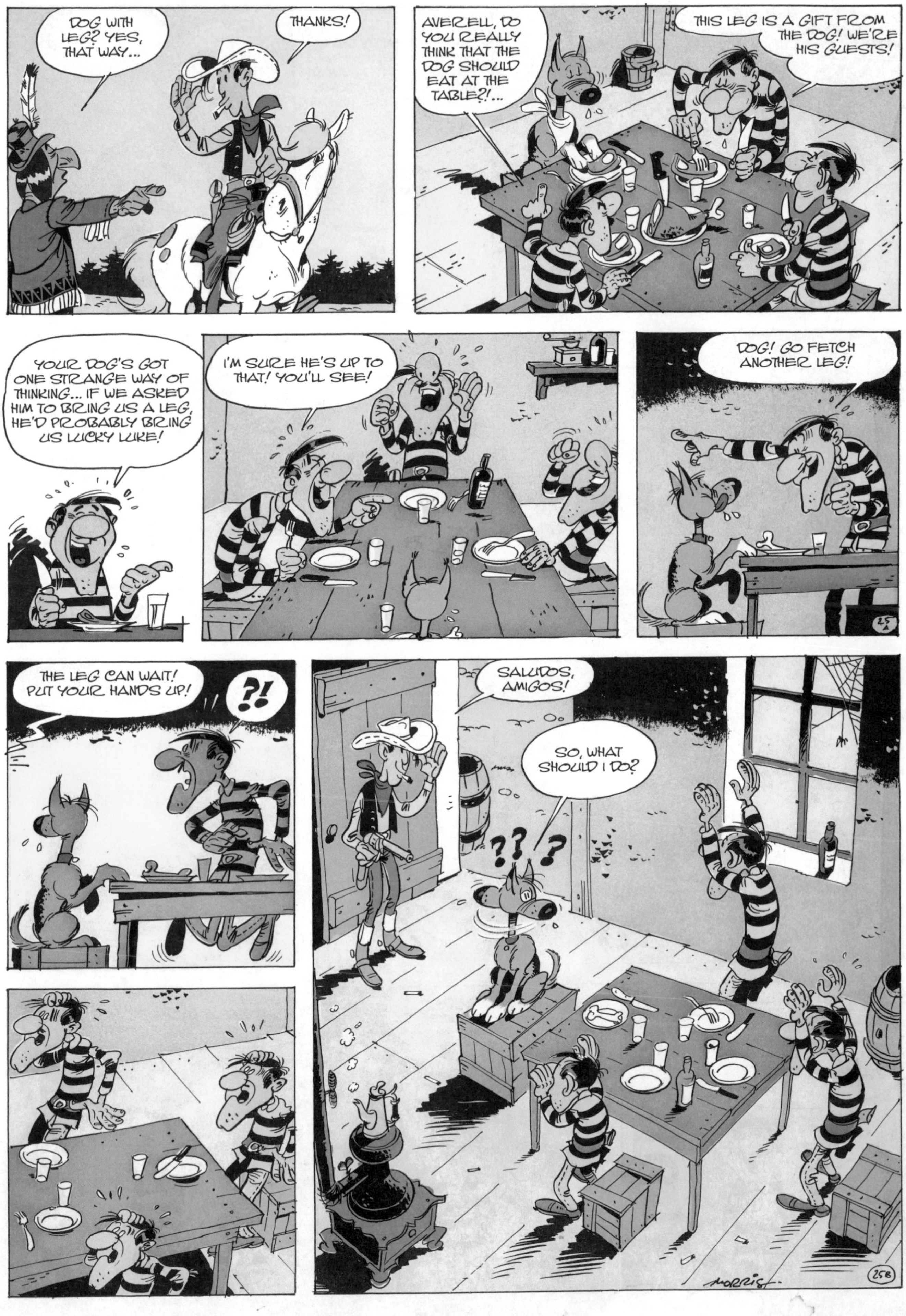
DOG WITH LEG? YES, THAT WAY...
THANKS!
AVERELL, DO YOU REALLY THINK THAT THE DOG SHOULD EAT AT THE TABLE?!...
THIS LEG IS A GIFT FROM THE DOG! WE'RE HIS GUESTS!
YOUR DOG'S GOT ONE STRANGE WAY OF THINKING... IF WE ASKED HIM TO BRING US A LEG, HE'D PROBABLY BRING US LUCKY LUKE!
I'M SURE HE'S UP TO THAT! YOU'LL SEE!
DOG! GO FETCH ANOTHER LEG!
THE LEG CAN WAIT! PUT YOUR HANDS UP!
?!
SALUDOS, AMIGOS!
SO, WHAT SHOULD I DO?
???
MORRIS

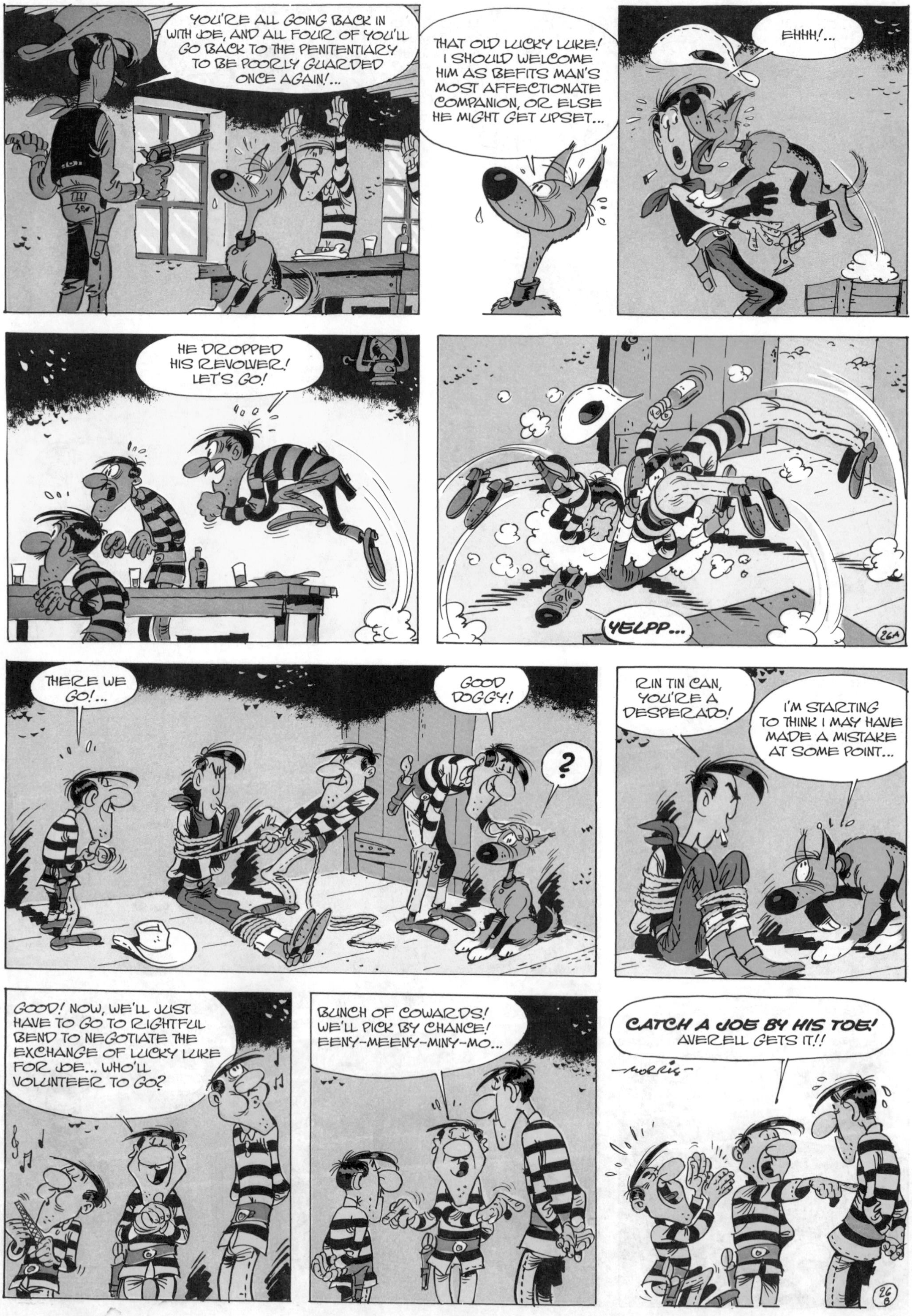
YOU'RE ALL GOING BACK IN WITH JOE, AND ALL FOUR OF YOU'LL GO BACK TO THE PENITENTIARY TO BE POORLY GUARDED ONCE AGAIN!...
THAT OLD LUCKY LUKE! I SHOULD WELCOME HIM AS BEFITS MAN'S MOST AFFECTIONATE COMPANION, OR ELSE HE MIGHT GET UPSET...
EHHH!...
HE DROPPED HIS REVOLVER! LET'S GO!
YELPP...
26A
THERE WE GO!...
GOOD DOGGY!
?
RIN TIN CAN, YOU'RE A DESPERADO!
I'M STARTING TO THINK I MAY HAVE MADE A MISTAKE AT SOME POINT...
GOOD! NOW, WE'LL JUST HAVE TO GO TO RIGHTFUL BEND TO NEGOTIATE THE EXCHANGE OF LUCKY LUKE FOR JOE... WHO'LL VOLUNTEER TO GO?
BUNCH OF COWARDS! WE'LL PICK BY CHANCE! EENY-MEENY-MINY-MO...
CATCH A JOE BY HIS TOE! AVERELL GETS IT!!
MORRIS
26B

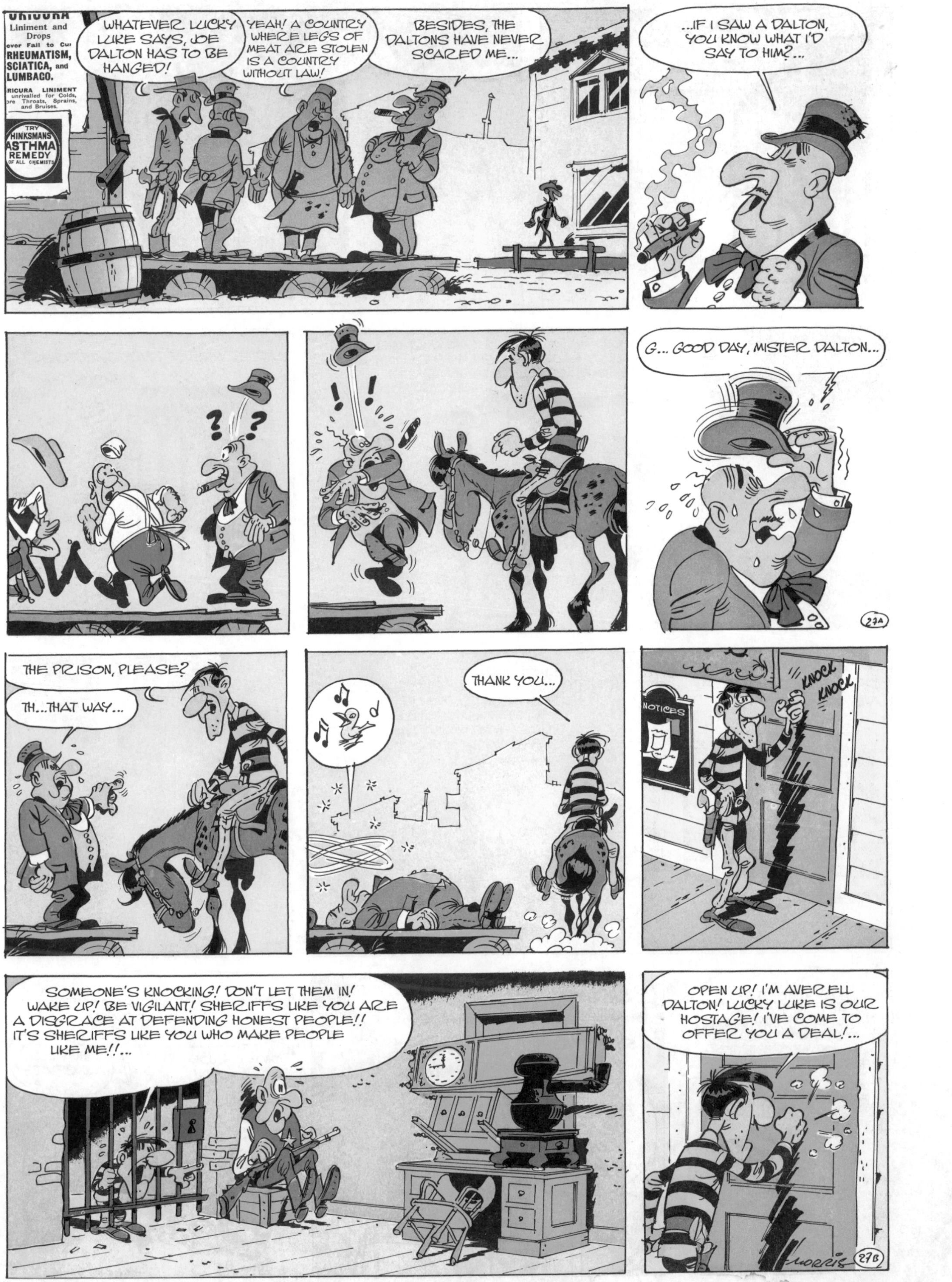
Liniment and Drops
RHEUMATISM, SCIATICA, and LUMBAGO.
unrivalled for Colds, Sprains, and Bruises.
TRY HINKSMANS ASTHMA REMEDY OF ALL CHEMISTS
WHATEVER LUCKY LUKE SAYS, JOE DALTON HAS TO BE HANGED!
YEAH! A COUNTRY WHERE LEGS OF MEAT ARE STOLEN IS A COUNTRY WITHOUT LAW!
BESIDES, THE DALTONS HAVE NEVER SCARED ME...
...IF I SAW A DALTON, YOU KNOW WHAT I'D SAY TO HIM?...
G... GOOD DAY, MISTER DALTON...
27A
THE PRISON, PLEASE?
TH...THAT WAY...
THANK YOU...
NOTICES
KNOCK KNOCK
SOMEONE'S KNOCKING! DON'T LET THEM IN! WAKE UP! BE VIGILANT! SHERIFFS LIKE YOU ARE A DISGRACE AT DEFENDING HONEST PEOPLE!! IT'S SHERIFFS LIKE YOU WHO MAKE PEOPLE LIKE ME!!...
OPEN UP! I'M AVERELL DALTON! LUCKY LUKE IS OUR HOSTAGE! I'VE COME TO OFFER YOU A DEAL!...
MORRIS
27B

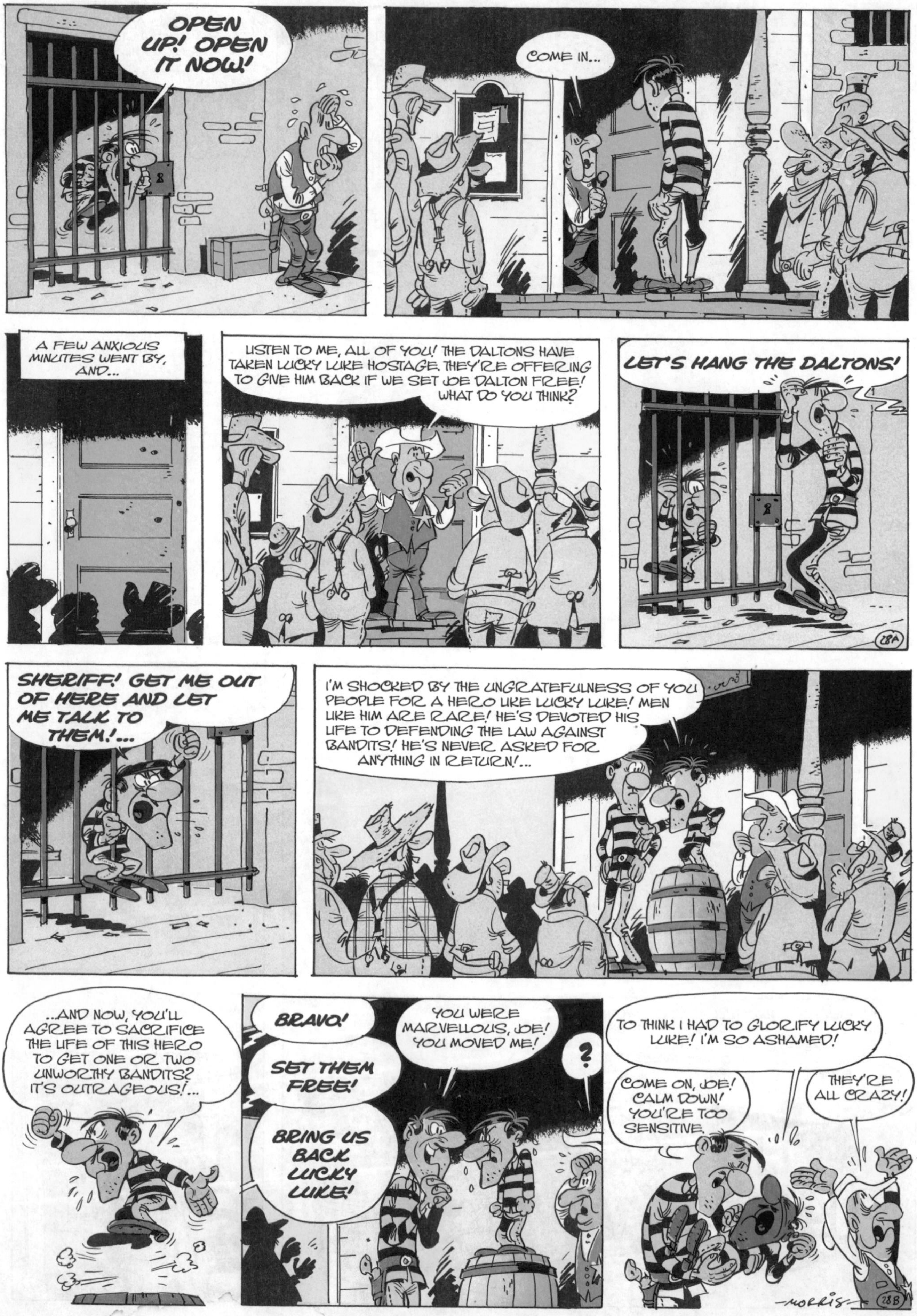
OPEN UP! OPEN IT NOW!
COME IN...
A FEW ANXIOUS MINUTES WENT BY, AND...
LISTEN TO ME, ALL OF YOU! THE DALTONS HAVE TAKEN LUCKY LUKE HOSTAGE. THEY'RE OFFERING TO GIVE HIM BACK IF WE SET JOE DALTON FREE! WHAT DO YOU THINK?
LET'S HANG THE DALTONS!
SHERIFF! GET ME OUT OF HERE AND LET ME TALK TO THEM!...
I'M SHOCKED BY THE UNGRATEFULNESS OF YOU PEOPLE FOR A HERO LIKE LUCKY LUKE! MEN LIKE HIM ARE RARE! HE'S DEVOTED HIS LIFE TO DEFENDING THE LAW AGAINST BANDITS! HE'S NEVER ASKED FOR ANYTHING IN RETURN!...
...AND NOW, YOU'LL AGREE TO SACRIFICE THE LIFE OF THIS HERO TO GET ONE OR TWO UNWORTHY BANDITS? IT'S OUTRAGEOUS!...
BRAVO!
SET THEM FREE!
BRING US BACK LUCKY LUKE!
YOU WERE MARVELLOUS, JOE! YOU MOVED ME!
?
TO THINK I HAD TO GLORIFY LUCKY LUKE! I'M SO ASHAMED!
COME ON, JOE! CALM DOWN! YOU'RE TOO SENSITIVE.
THEY'RE ALL CRAZY!
MORRIS

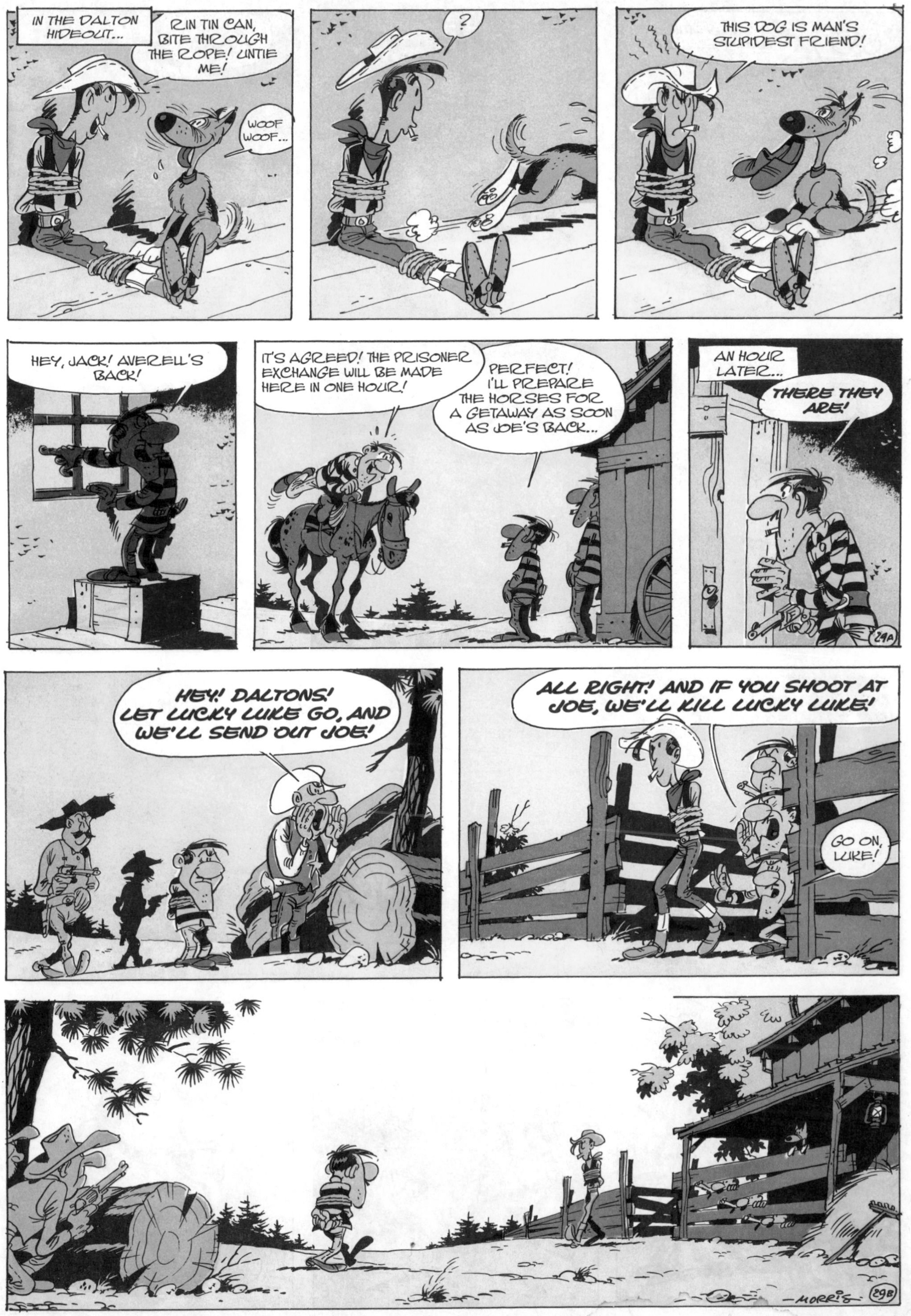
IN THE DALTON HIDEOUT...
RIN TIN CAN, BITE THROUGH THE ROPE! UNTIE ME!
WOOF WOOF...
?
THIS DOG IS MAN'S STUPIDEST FRIEND!
HEY, JACK! AVERELL'S BACK!
IT'S AGREED! THE PRISONER EXCHANGE WILL BE MADE HERE IN ONE HOUR!
PERFECT! I'LL PREPARE THE HORSES FOR A GETAWAY AS SOON AS JOE'S BACK...
AN HOUR LATER...
THERE THEY ARE!
HEY! DALTONS! LET LUCKY LUKE GO, AND WE'LL SEND OUT JOE!
ALL RIGHT! AND IF YOU SHOOT AT JOE, WE'LL KILL LUCKY LUKE!
GO ON, LUKE!
MORRIS

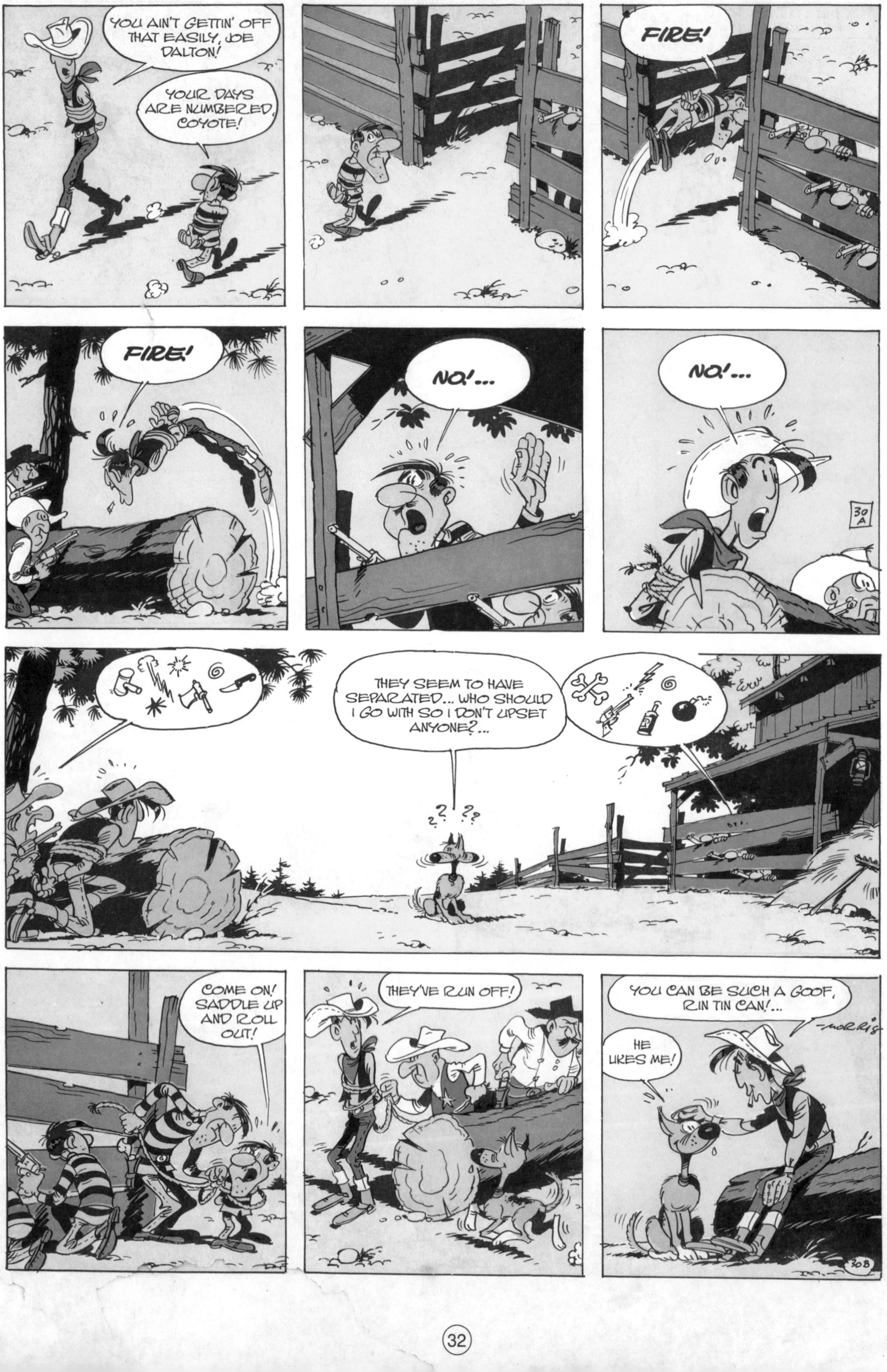
YOU AIN'T GETTIN' OFF THAT EASILY, JOE DALTON!
YOUR DAYS ARE NUMBERED, COYOTE!
FIRE!
FIRE!
NO!...
NO!...
30 A
THEY SEEM TO HAVE SEPARATED... WHO SHOULD I GO WITH SO I DON'T UPSET ANYONE?...
COME ON! SADDLE UP AND ROLL OUT!
THEY'VE RUN OFF!
YOU CAN BE SUCH A GOOF, RIN TIN CAN!...
HE LIKES ME!
MORRIS
30 B

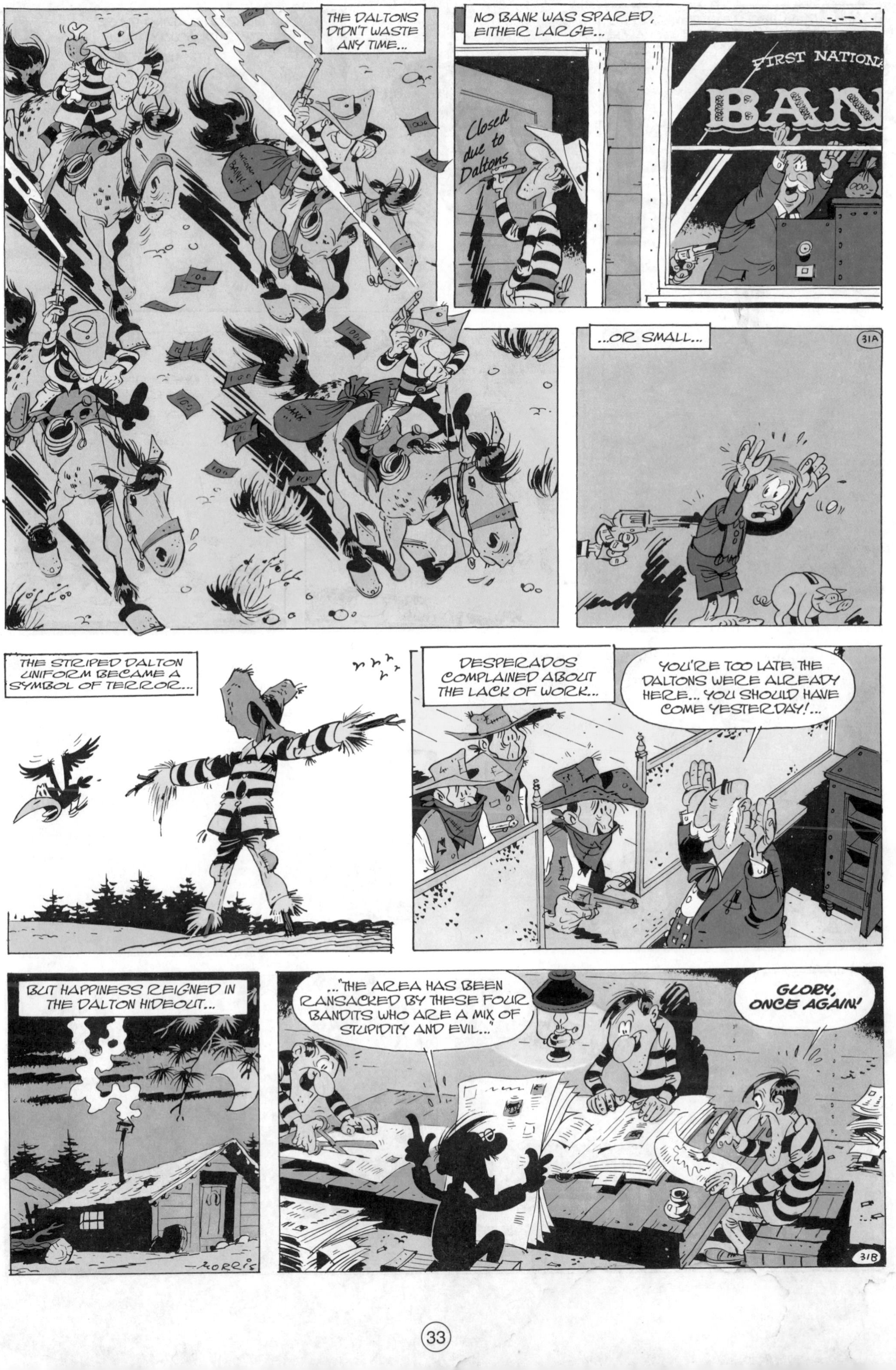
THE DALTONS DIDN'T WASTE ANY TIME...
NO BANK WAS SPARED, EITHER LARGE...
FIRST NATIONA
BAN
Closed due to Daltons
...OR SMALL...
31A
THE STRIPED DALTON UNIFORM BECAME A SYMBOL OF TERROR...
DESPERADOS COMPLAINED ABOUT THE LACK OF WORK...
YOU'RE TOO LATE. THE DALTONS WERE ALREADY HERE... YOU SHOULD HAVE COME YESTERDAY!...
BUT HAPPINESS REIGNED IN THE DALTON HIDEOUT...
MORRIS
..."THE AREA HAS BEEN RANSACKED BY THESE FOUR BANDITS WHO ARE A MIX OF STUPIDITY AND EVIL..."
GLORY, ONCE AGAIN!
31B

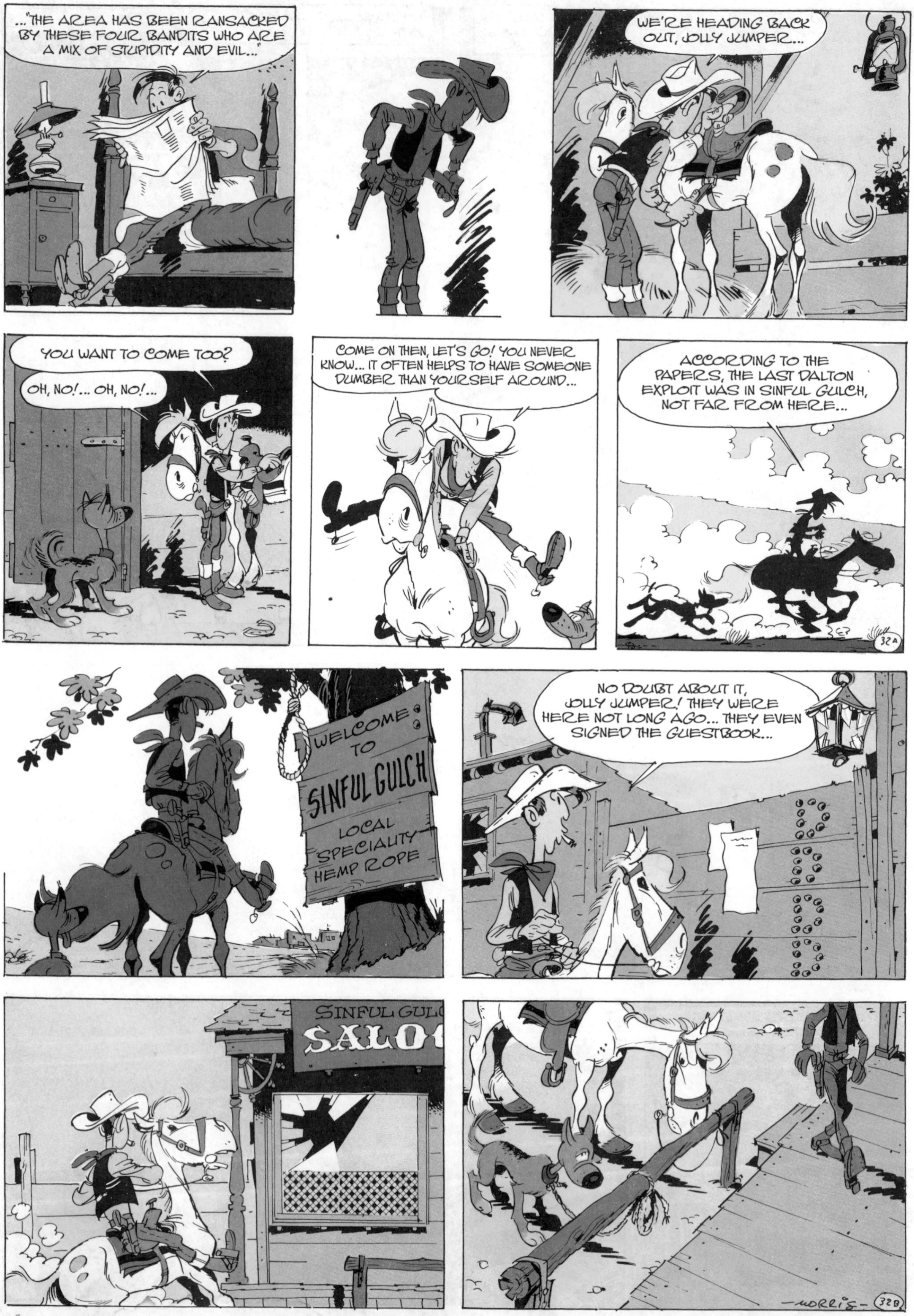
..."THE AREA HAS BEEN RANSACKED BY THESE FOUR BANDITS WHO ARE A MIX OF STUPIDITY AND EVIL..."
WE'RE HEADING BACK OUT, JOLLY JUMPER...
YOU WANT TO COME TOO?
OH, NO!... OH, NO!...
COME ON THEN, LET'S GO! YOU NEVER KNOW... IT OFTEN HELPS TO HAVE SOMEONE DUMBER THAN YOURSELF AROUND...
ACCORDING TO THE PAPERS, THE LAST DALTON EXPLOIT WAS IN SINFUL GULCH, NOT FAR FROM HERE...
32A
WELCOME TO SINFUL GULCH LOCAL SPECIALITY HEMP ROPE
NO DOUBT ABOUT IT, JOLLY JUMPER! THEY WERE HERE NOT LONG AGO... THEY EVEN SIGNED THE GUESTBOOK...
SINFUL GULC
SALO
MORRIS
32B

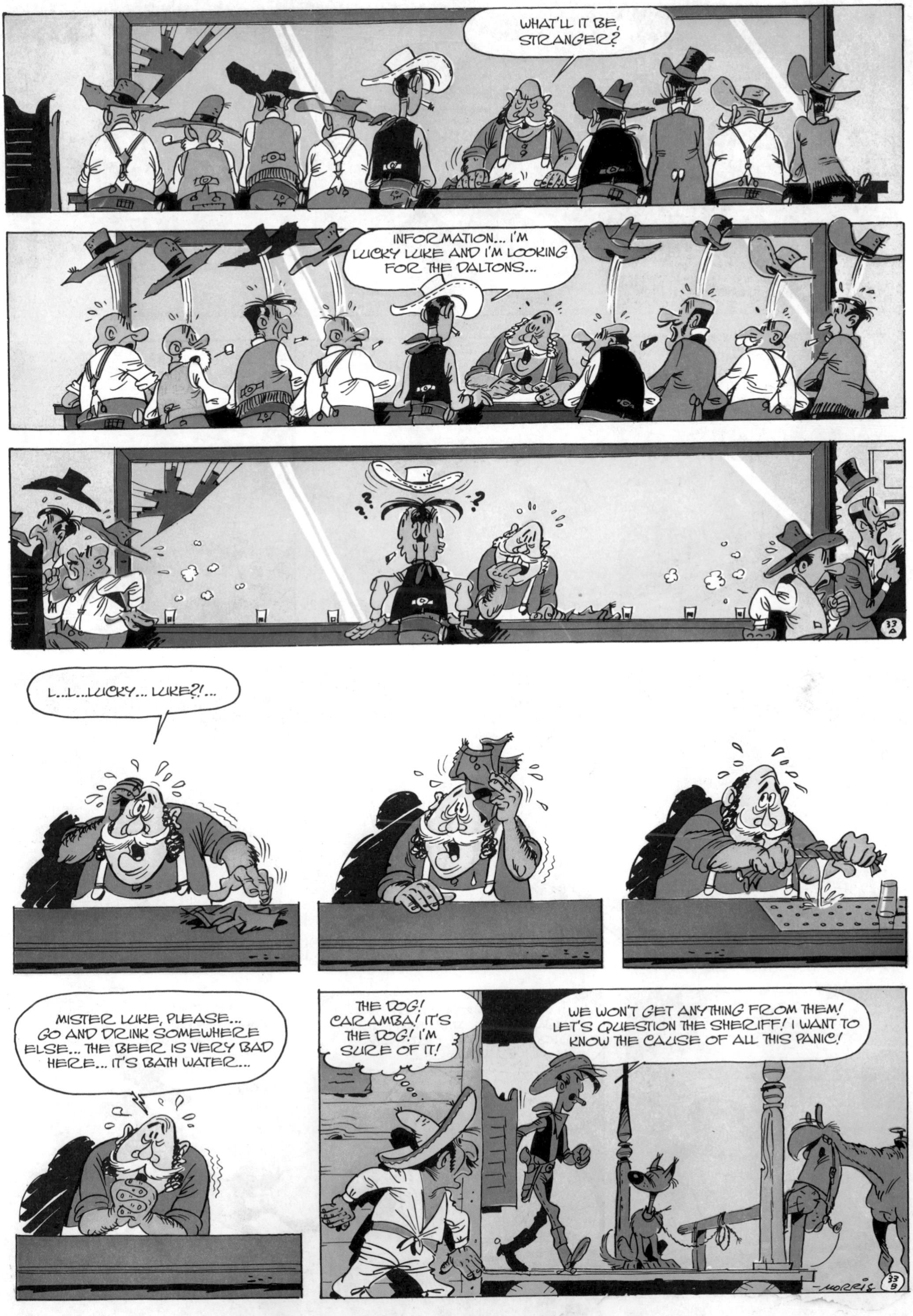
WHAT'LL IT BE, STRANGER?
INFORMATION... I'M LUCKY LUKE AND I'M LOOKING FOR THE DALTONS...
L...L...LUCKY... LUKE?!...
MISTER LUKE, PLEASE... GO AND DRINK SOMEWHERE ELSE... THE BEER IS VERY BAD HERE... IT'S BATH WATER...
THE DOG! CARAMBA! IT'S THE DOG! I'M SURE OF IT!
WE WON'T GET ANYTHING FROM THEM! LET'S QUESTION THE SHERIFF! I WANT TO KNOW THE CAUSE OF ALL THIS PANIC!
MORRIS

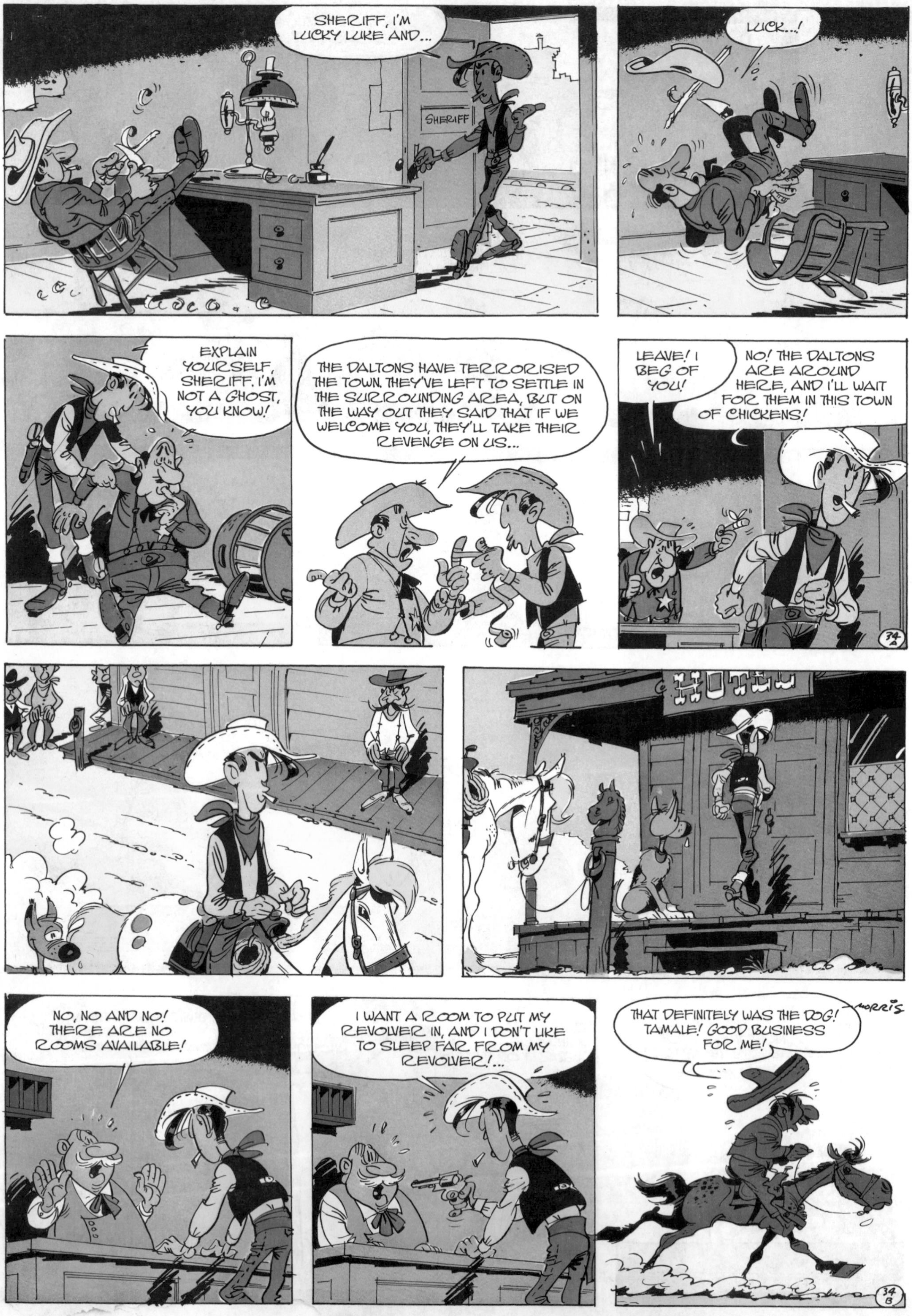
SHERIFF, I'M LUCKY LUKE AND...
SHERIFF
LUCK...!
EXPLAIN YOURSELF, SHERIFF. I'M NOT A GHOST, YOU KNOW!
THE DALTONS HAVE TERRORISED THE TOWN. THEY'VE LEFT TO SETTLE IN THE SURROUNDING AREA, BUT ON THE WAY OUT THEY SAID THAT IF WE WELCOME YOU, THEY'LL TAKE THEIR REVENGE ON US...
LEAVE! I BEG OF YOU!
NO! THE DALTONS ARE AROUND HERE, AND I'LL WAIT FOR THEM IN THIS TOWN OF CHICKENS!
NO, NO AND NO! THERE ARE NO ROOMS AVAILABLE!
I WANT A ROOM TO PUT MY REVOLVER IN, AND I DON'T LIKE TO SLEEP FAR FROM MY REVOLVER!...
THAT DEFINITELY WAS THE DOG! TAMALE! GOOD BUSINESS FOR ME!
MORRIS

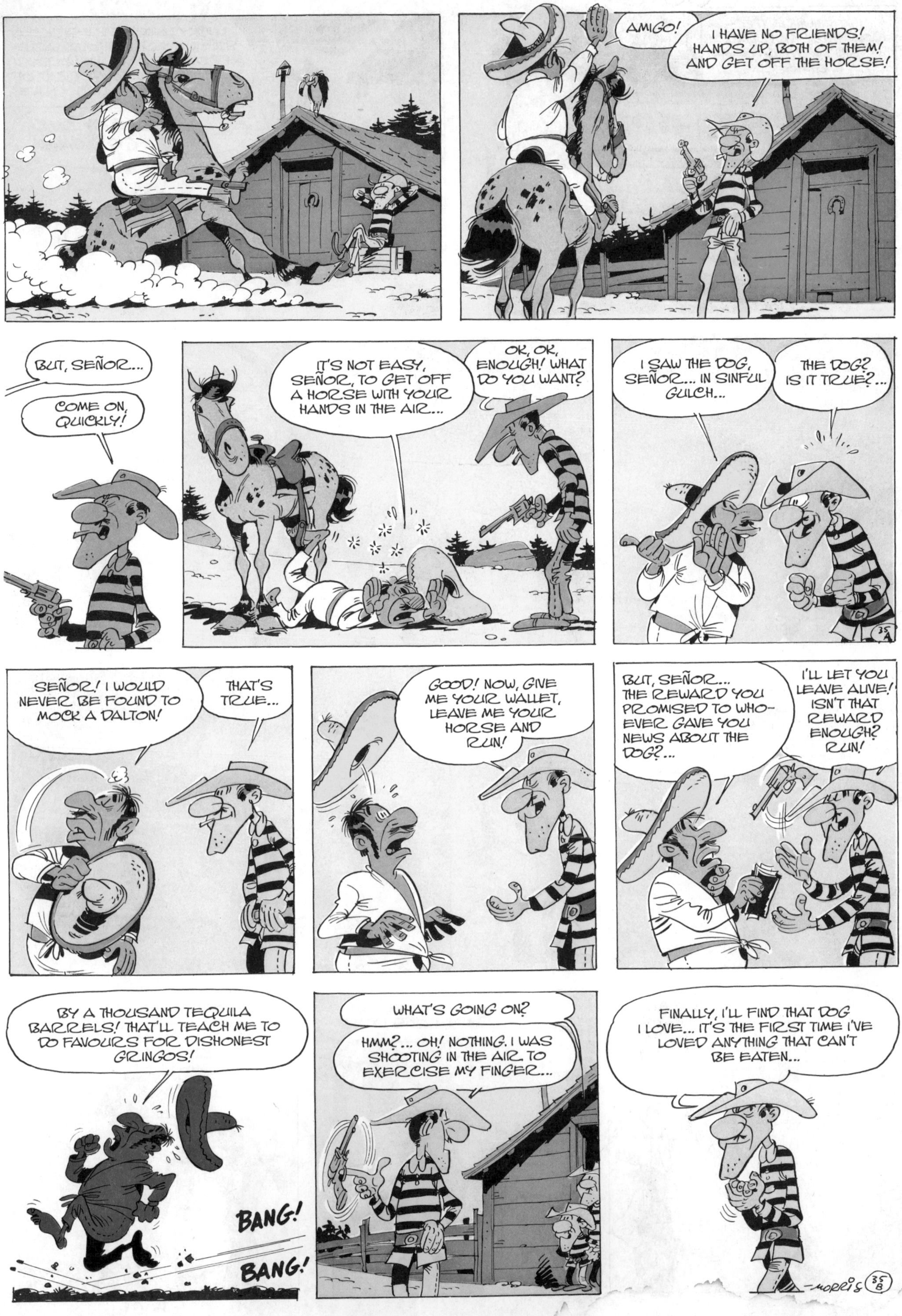

AMIGO!
I HAVE NO FRIENDS! HANDS UP, BOTH OF THEM! AND GET OFF THE HORSE!
BUT, SEÑOR...
COME ON, QUICKLY!
IT'S NOT EASY, SEÑOR, TO GET OFF A HORSE WITH YOUR HANDS IN THE AIR...
OK, OK, ENOUGH! WHAT DO YOU WANT?
I SAW THE DOG, SEÑOR... IN SINFUL GULCH...
THE DOG? IS IT TRUE?...
SEÑOR! I WOULD NEVER BE FOUND TO MOCK A DALTON!
THAT'S TRUE...
GOOD! NOW, GIVE ME YOUR WALLET, LEAVE ME YOUR HORSE AND RUN!
BUT, SEÑOR... THE REWARD YOU PROMISED TO WHO-EVER GAVE YOU NEWS ABOUT THE DOG?...
I'LL LET YOU LEAVE ALIVE! ISN'T THAT REWARD ENOUGH? RUN!
BY A THOUSAND TEQUILA BARRELS! THAT'LL TEACH ME TO DO FAVOURS FOR DISHONEST GRINGOS!
BANG!
BANG!
WHAT'S GOING ON?
HMM?... OH! NOTHING. I WAS SHOOTING IN THE AIR TO EXERCISE MY FINGER...
FINALLY, I'LL FIND THAT DOG I LOVE... IT'S THE FIRST TIME I'VE LOVED ANYTHING THAT CAN'T BE EATEN...
MORRIS

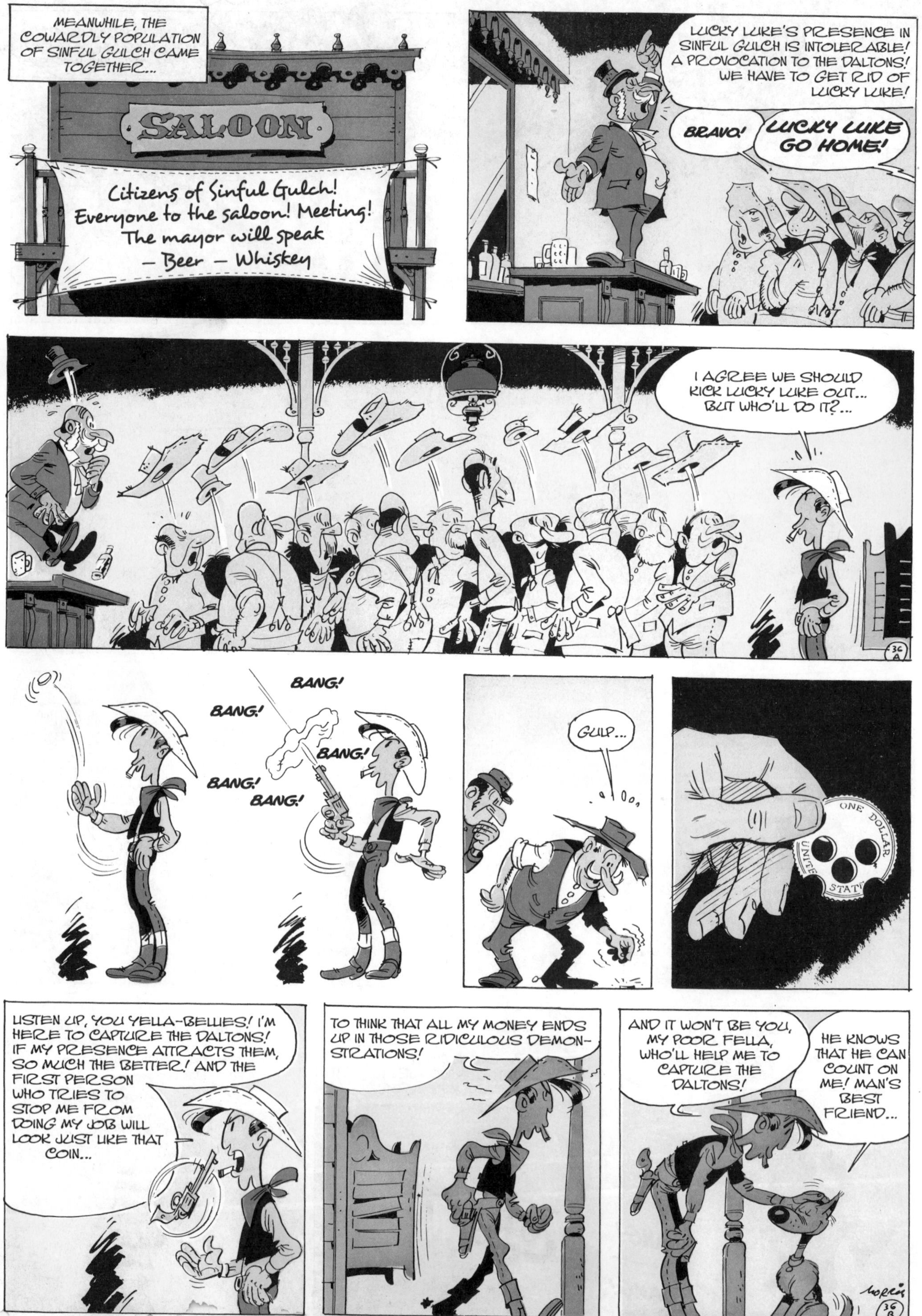
MEANWHILE, THE COWARDLY POPULATION OF SINFUL GULCH CAME TOGETHER...
SALOON
Citizens of Sinful Gulch! Everyone to the saloon! Meeting! The mayor will speak — Beer — Whiskey
LUCKY LUKE'S PRESENCE IN SINFUL GULCH IS INTOLERABLE! A PROVOCATION TO THE DALTONS! WE HAVE TO GET RID OF LUCKY LUKE!
BRAVO!
LUCKY LUKE GO HOME!
I AGREE WE SHOULD KICK LUCKY LUKE OUT... BUT WHO'LL DO IT?...
BANG!
BANG!
BANG!
BANG!
BANG!
GULP...
ONE DOLLAR
UNITED STATES
LISTEN UP, YOU YELLA-BELLIES! I'M HERE TO CAPTURE THE DALTONS! IF MY PRESENCE ATTRACTS THEM, SO MUCH THE BETTER! AND THE FIRST PERSON WHO TRIES TO STOP ME FROM DOING MY JOB WILL LOOK JUST LIKE THAT COIN...
TO THINK THAT ALL MY MONEY ENDS UP IN THOSE RIDICULOUS DEMONSTRATIONS!
AND IT WON'T BE YOU, MY POOR FELLA, WHO'LL HELP ME TO CAPTURE THE DALTONS!
HE KNOWS THAT HE CAN COUNT ON ME! MAN'S BEST FRIEND...
morris

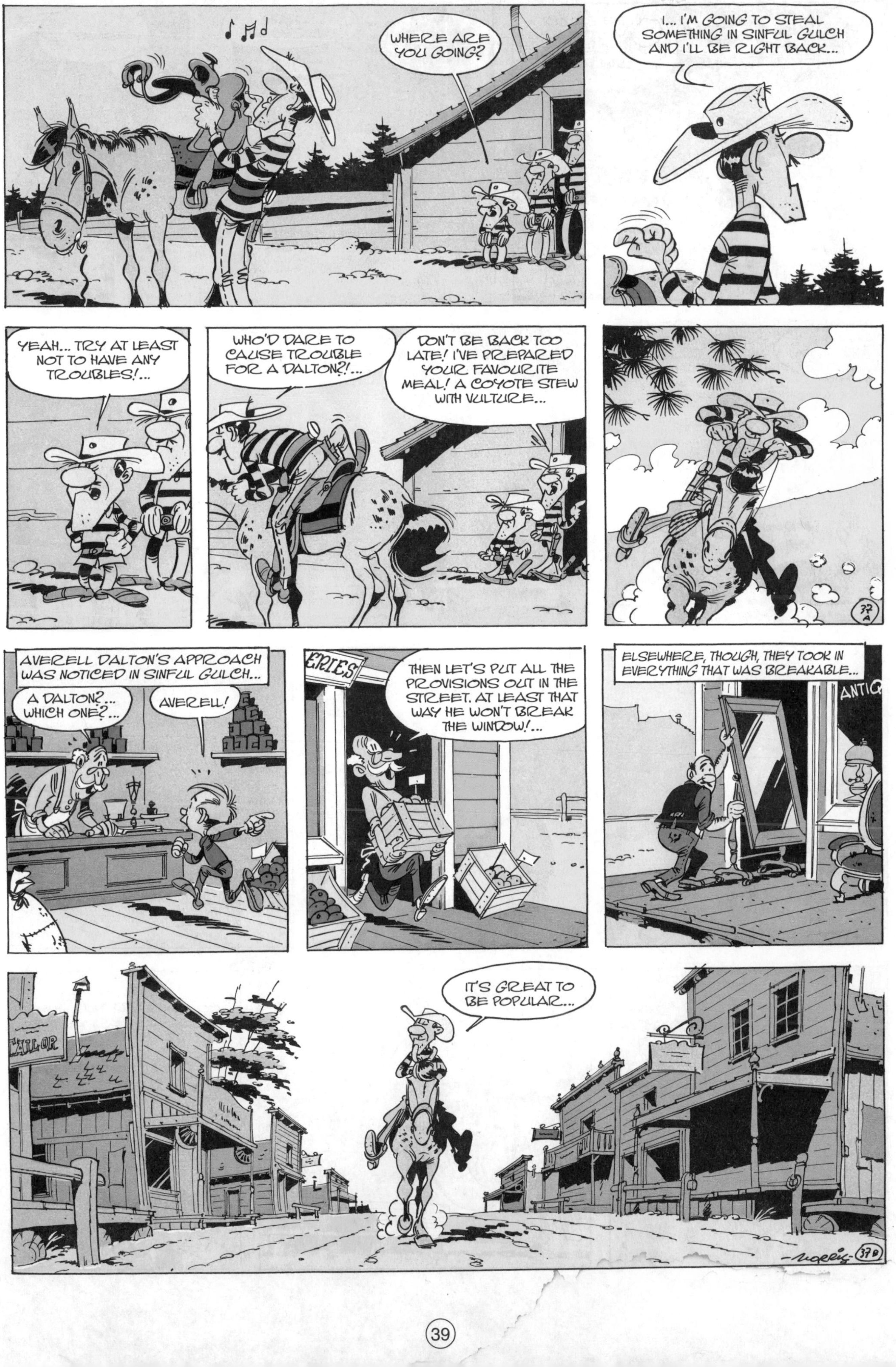
WHERE ARE YOU GOING?
I... I'M GOING TO STEAL SOMETHING IN SINFUL GULCH AND I'LL BE RIGHT BACK...
YEAH... TRY AT LEAST NOT TO HAVE ANY TROUBLES!...
WHO'D DARE TO CAUSE TROUBLE FOR A DALTON?!...
DON'T BE BACK TOO LATE! I'VE PREPARED YOUR FAVOURITE MEAL! A COYOTE STEW WITH VULTURE...
AVERELL DALTON'S APPROACH WAS NOTICED IN SINFUL GULCH...
A DALTON?... WHICH ONE?...
AVERELL!
ERIES
THEN LET'S PUT ALL THE PROVISIONS OUT IN THE STREET. AT LEAST THAT WAY HE WON'T BREAK THE WINDOW!...
ELSEWHERE, THOUGH, THEY TOOK IN EVERYTHING THAT WAS BREAKABLE...
ANTIQ
IT'S GREAT TO BE POPULAR...
TAILOR
MORRIS

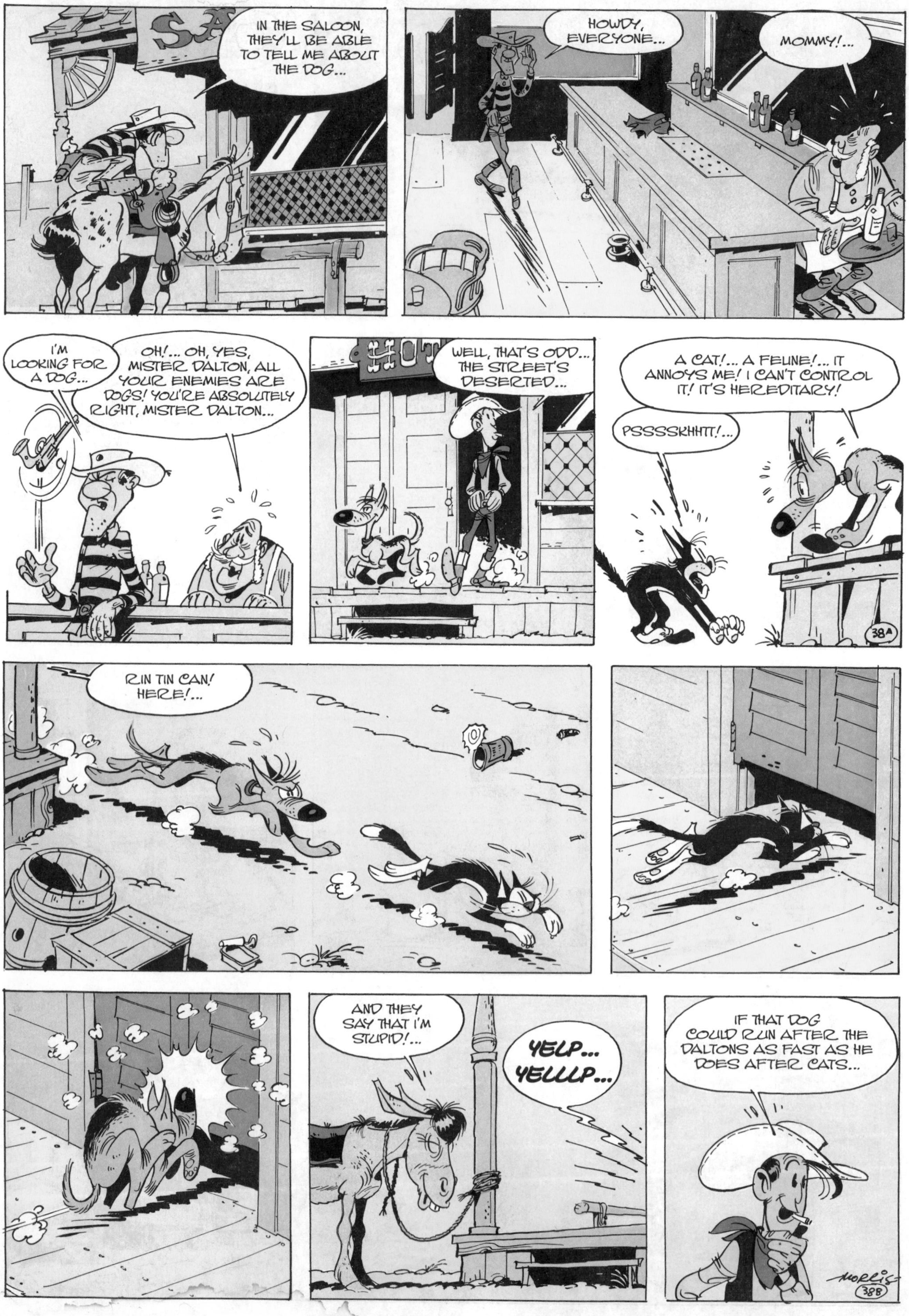

IN THE SALOON, THEY'LL BE ABLE TO TELL ME ABOUT THE DOG...
HOWDY, EVERYONE...
MOMMY!...
I'M LOOKING FOR A DOG...
OH!... OH, YES, MISTER DALTON, ALL YOUR ENEMIES ARE DOGS! YOU'RE ABSOLUTELY RIGHT, MISTER DALTON...
WELL, THAT'S ODD... THE STREET'S DESERTED...
A CAT!... A FELINE!... IT ANNOYS ME! I CAN'T CONTROL IT! IT'S HEREDITARY!
PSSSSKHHTT!...
38A
RIN TIN CAN! HERE!...
AND THEY SAY THAT I'M STUPID!...
YELP... YELLLP...
IF THAT DOG COULD RUN AFTER THE DALTONS AS FAST AS HE DOES AFTER CATS...
MORRIS
38B

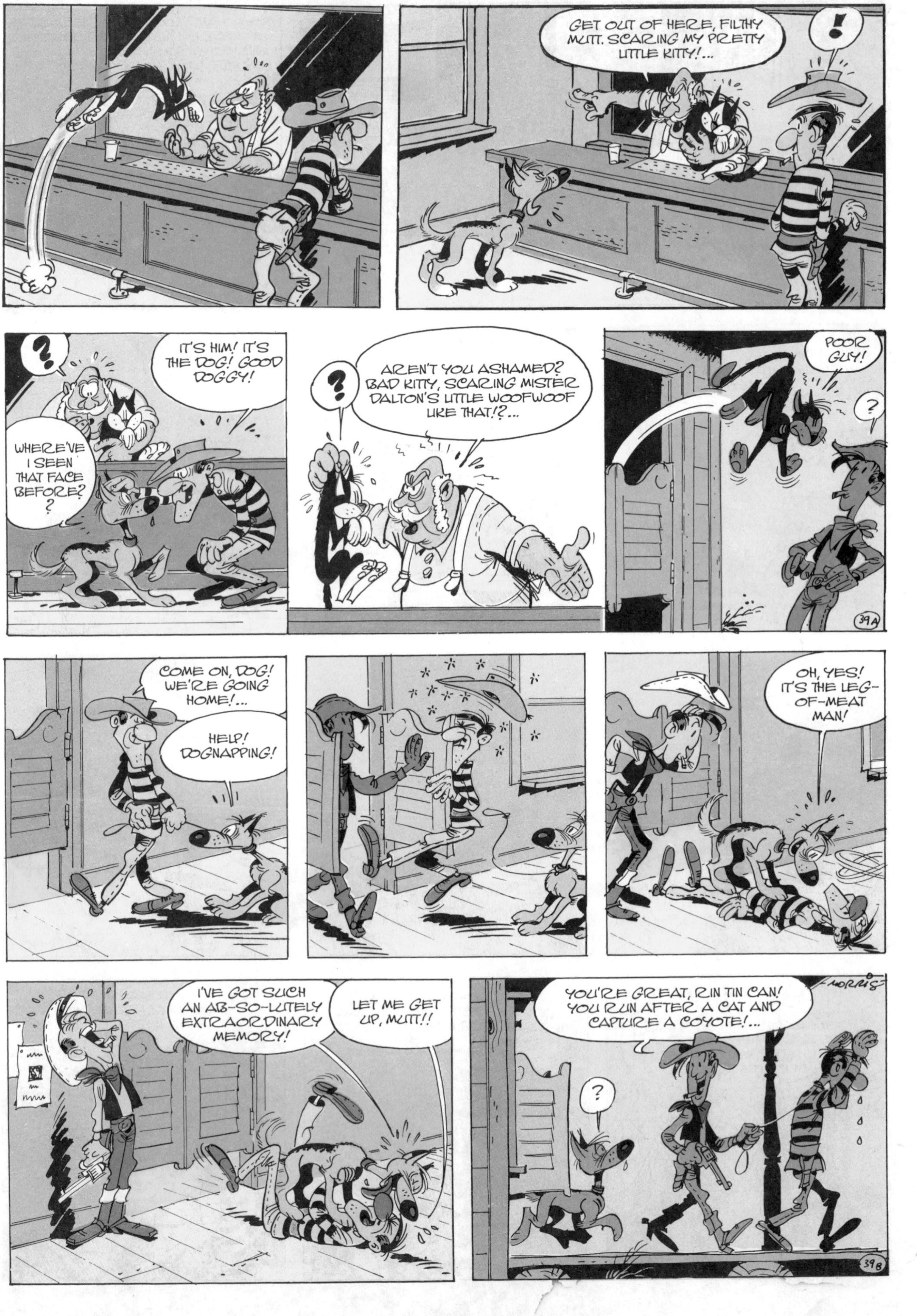
GET OUT OF HERE, FILTHY MUTT. SCARING MY PRETTY LITTLE KITTY!...
!
?
IT'S HIM! IT'S THE DOG! GOOD DOGGY!
WHERE'VE I SEEN THAT FACE BEFORE? ?
?
AREN'T YOU ASHAMED? BAD KITTY, SCARING MISTER DALTON'S LITTLE WOOFWOOF LIKE THAT!?...
POOR GUY!
?
39A
COME ON, DOG! WE'RE GOING HOME!...
HELP! DOGNAPPING!
OH, YES! IT'S THE LEG-OF-MEAT MAN!
I'VE GOT SUCH AN AB-SO-LUTELY EXTRAORDINARY MEMORY!
LET ME GET UP, MUTT!!
MORRIS
YOU'RE GREAT, RIN TIN CAN! YOU RUN AFTER A CAT AND CAPTURE A COYOTE!...
?
39B

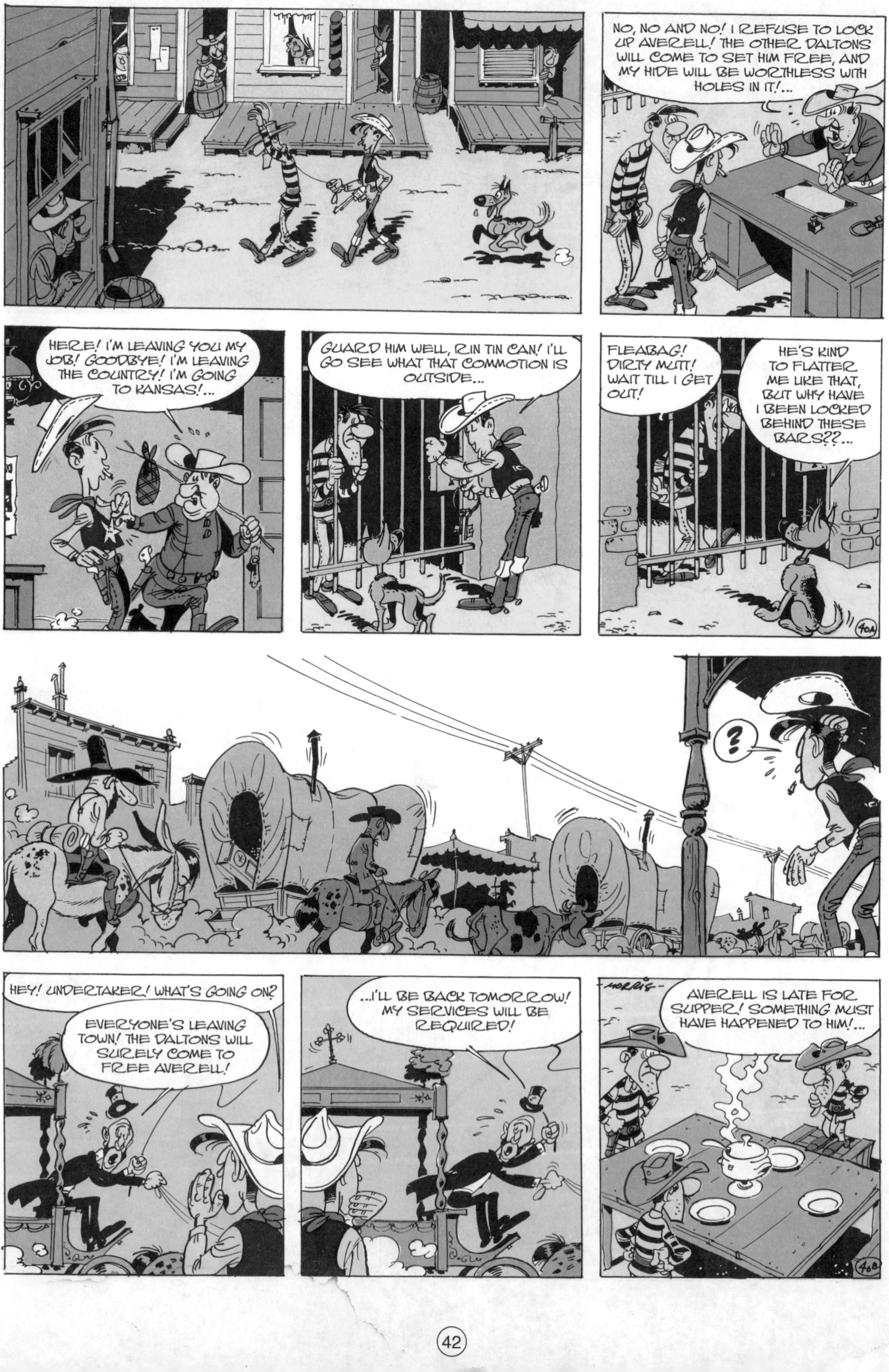

NO, NO AND NO! I REFUSE TO LOCK UP AVERELL! THE OTHER DALTONS WILL COME TO SET HIM FREE, AND MY HIDE WILL BE WORTHLESS WITH HOLES IN IT!...
HERE! I'M LEAVING YOU MY JOB! GOODBYE! I'M LEAVING THE COUNTRY! I'M GOING TO KANSAS!...
GUARD HIM WELL, RIN TIN CAN! I'LL GO SEE WHAT THAT COMMOTION IS OUTSIDE...
FLEABAG! DIRTY MUTT! WAIT TILL I GET OUT!
HE'S KIND TO FLATTER ME LIKE THAT, BUT WHY HAVE I BEEN LOCKED BEHIND THESE BARS??...
?
HEY! UNDERTAKER! WHAT'S GOING ON?
EVERYONE'S LEAVING TOWN! THE DALTONS WILL SURELY COME TO FREE AVERELL!
...I'LL BE BACK TOMORROW! MY SERVICES WILL BE REQUIRED!
MORRIS
AVERELL IS LATE FOR SUPPER! SOMETHING MUST HAVE HAPPENED TO HIM!...

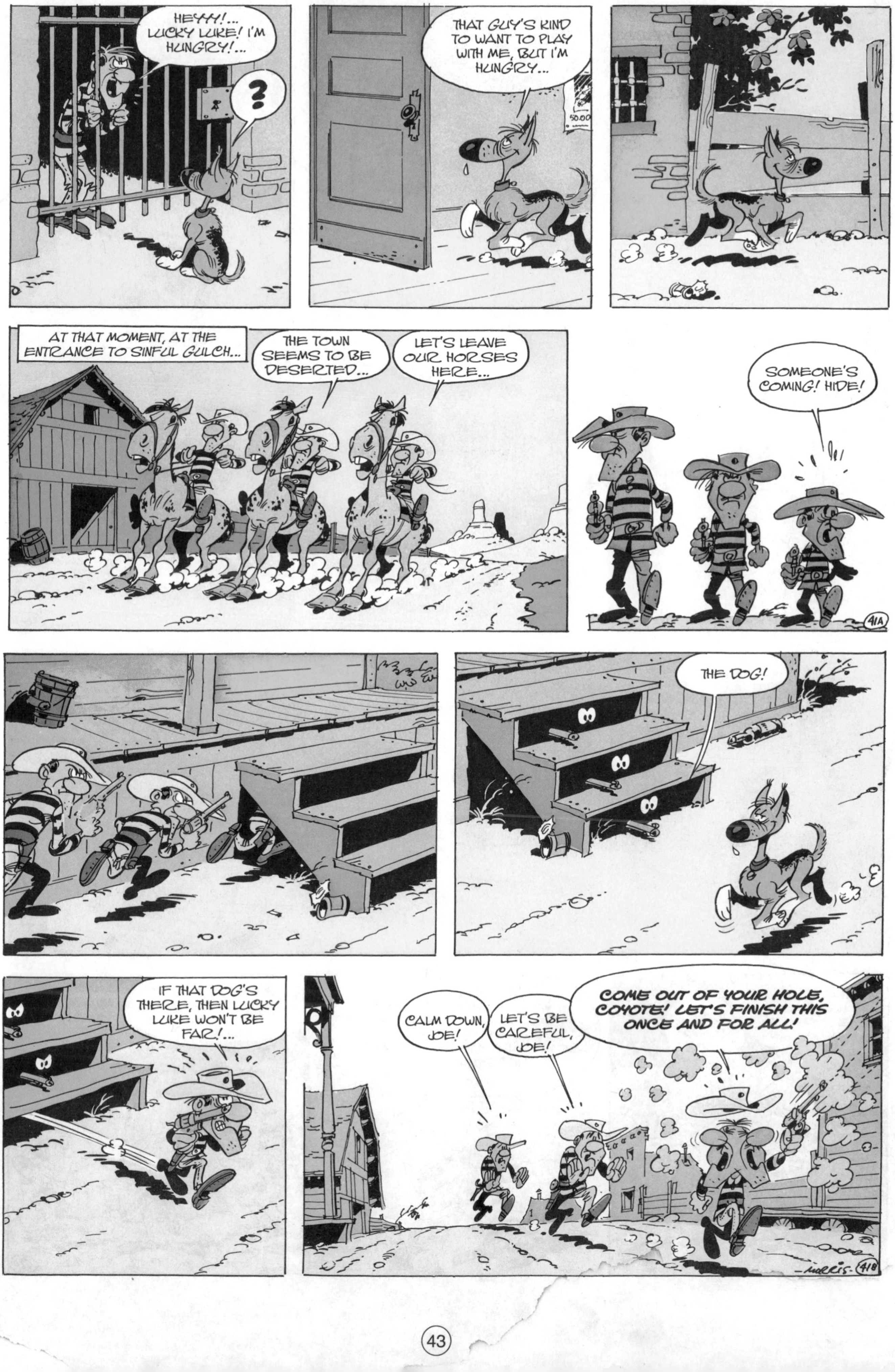
HEYYY!... LUCKY LUKE! I'M HUNGRY!...
?
THAT GUY'S KIND TO WANT TO PLAY WITH ME, BUT I'M HUNGRY...
AT THAT MOMENT, AT THE ENTRANCE TO SINFUL GULCH...
THE TOWN SEEMS TO BE DESERTED...
LET'S LEAVE OUR HORSES HERE...
SOMEONE'S COMING! HIDE!
THE DOG!
IF THAT DOG'S THERE, THEN LUCKY LUKE WON'T BE FAR!...
CALM DOWN, JOE!
LET'S BE CAREFUL, JOE!
COME OUT OF YOUR HOLE, COYOTE! LET'S FINISH THIS ONCE AND FOR ALL!

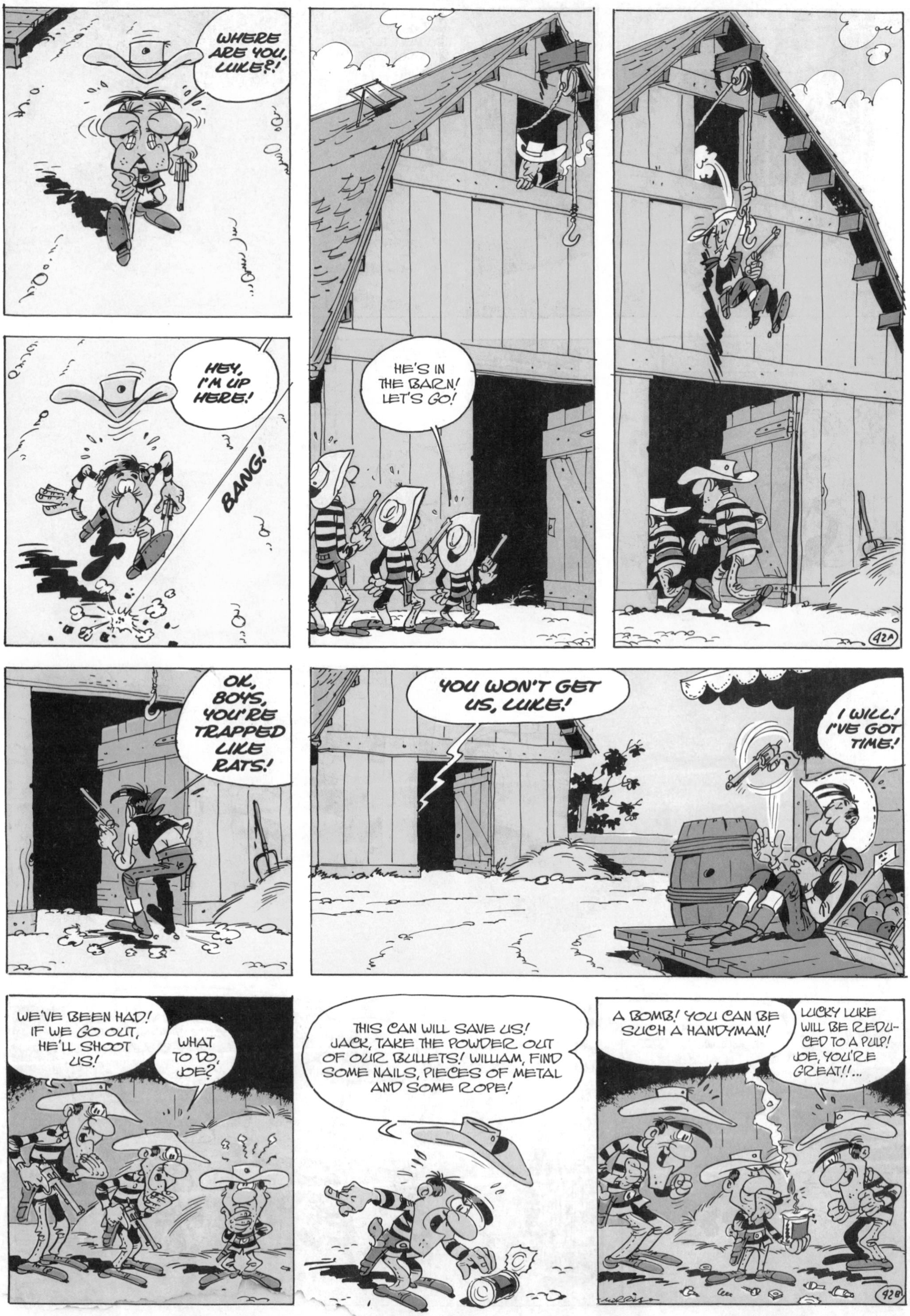
WHERE ARE YOU, LUKE?!
HEY, I'M UP HERE!
BANG!
HE'S IN THE BARN! LET'S GO!
OK, BOYS, YOU'RE TRAPPED LIKE RATS!
YOU WON'T GET US, LUKE!
I WILL! I'VE GOT TIME!
WE'VE BEEN HAD! IF WE GO OUT, HE'LL SHOOT US!
WHAT TO DO, JOE?
THIS CAN WILL SAVE US! JACK, TAKE THE POWDER OUT OF OUR BULLETS! WILLIAM, FIND SOME NAILS, PIECES OF METAL AND SOME ROPE!
A BOMB! YOU CAN BE SUCH A HANDYMAN!
LUCKY LUKE WILL BE REDUCED TO A PULP! JOE, YOU'RE GREAT!!...

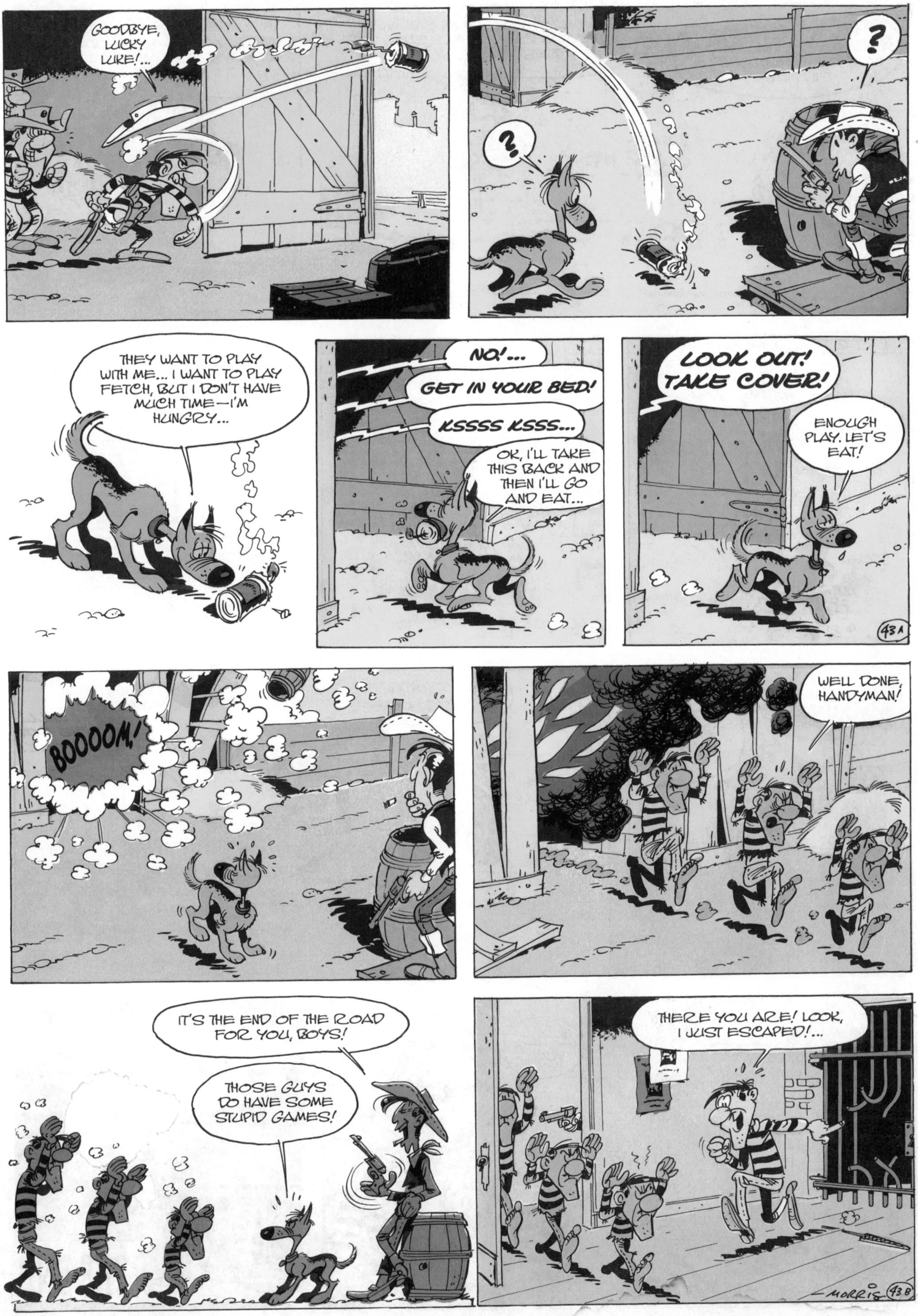

GOODBYE, LUCKY LUKE!...
?
?
THEY WANT TO PLAY WITH ME... I WANT TO PLAY FETCH, BUT I DON'T HAVE MUCH TIME—I'M HUNGRY...
NO!...
GET IN YOUR BED!
KSSSS KSSS...
OK, I'LL TAKE THIS BACK AND THEN I'LL GO AND EAT...
LOOK OUT! TAKE COVER!
ENOUGH PLAY. LET'S EAT!
43A
BOOOOM!
WELL DONE, HANDYMAN!
IT'S THE END OF THE ROAD FOR YOU, BOYS!
THOSE GUYS DO HAVE SOME STUPID GAMES!
THERE YOU ARE! LOOK, I JUST ESCAPED!...
MORRIS
43B

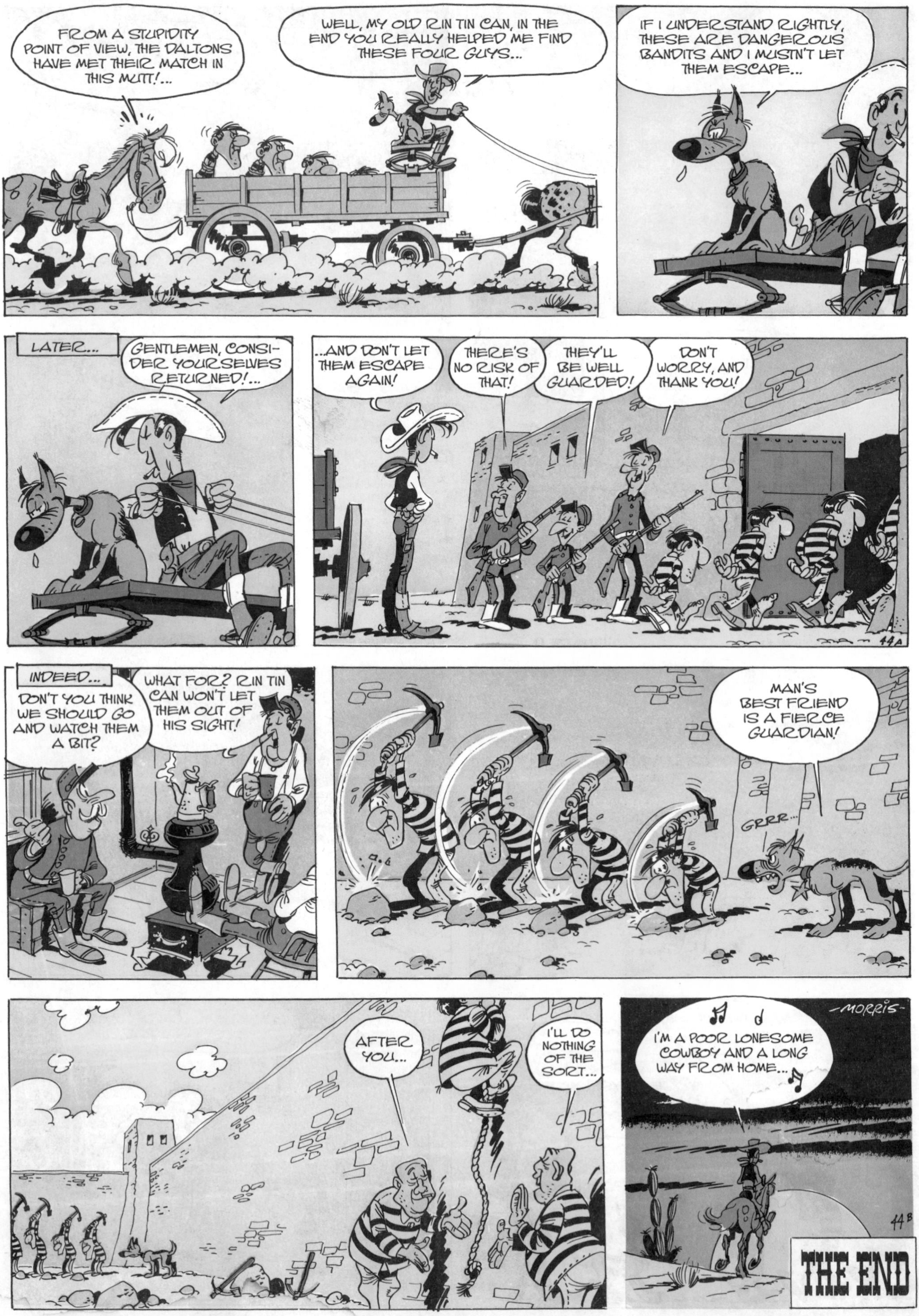
FROM A STUPIDITY POINT OF VIEW, THE DALTONS HAVE MET THEIR MATCH IN THIS MUTT!...
WELL, MY OLD RIN TIN CAN, IN THE END YOU REALLY HELPED ME FIND THESE FOUR GUYS...
IF I UNDERSTAND RIGHTLY, THESE ARE DANGEROUS BANDITS AND I MUSTN'T LET THEM ESCAPE...
LATER...
GENTLEMEN, CONSIDER YOURSELVES RETURNED!...
...AND DON'T LET THEM ESCAPE AGAIN!
THERE'S NO RISK OF THAT!
THEY'LL BE WELL GUARDED!
DON'T WORRY, AND THANK YOU!
44A
INDEED...
DON'T YOU THINK WE SHOULD GO AND WATCH THEM A BIT?
WHAT FOR? RIN TIN CAN WON'T LET THEM OUT OF HIS SIGHT!
MAN'S BEST FRIEND IS A FIERCE GUARDIAN!
GRRR...
AFTER YOU...
I'LL DO NOTHING OF THE SORT...
-MORRIS-
I'M A POOR LONESOME COWBOY AND A LONG WAY FROM HOME...
44B
THE END

LUCKY LUKE

The man who shoots faster than his own shadow

A LUCKY LUKE ADVENTURE 1
BILLY the Kid

A LUCKY LUKE ADVENTURE 2
GHOST TOWN

A LUCKY LUKE ADVENTURE 3
DALTON CITY

A LUCKY LUKE ADVENTURE 4
JESSE JAMES

A LUCKY LUKE ADVENTURE 5
IN THE SHADOW OF THE DERRICKS

A LUCKY LUKE ADVENTURE 6
MA DALTON

A LUCKY LUKE ADVENTURE 7
BARBED WIRE ON THE PRAIRIE

A LUCKY LUKE ADVENTURE 8
CALAMITY JANE

A LUCKY LUKE ADVENTURE 9
THE WAGON TRAIN

A LUCKY LUKE ADVENTURE 10
TORTILLAS FOR THE DALTONS

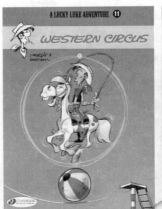

A LUCKY LUKE ADVENTURE 11
WESTERN CIRCUS

A LUCKY LUKE ADVENTURE 12
THE RIVALS OF PAINFUL GULCH

A LUCKY LUKE ADVENTURE 13
THE TENDERFOOT

A LUCKY LUKE ADVENTURE 14
THE DASHING WHITE COWBOY

A LUCKY LUKE ADVENTURE 15
THE DALTONS IN THE BLIZZARD

A LUCKY LUKE ADVENTURE 16
THE BLACK HILLS

COMING SOON

A LUCKY LUKE ADVENTURE 17
APACHE CANYON

A LUCKY LUKE ADVENTURE 18
THE ESCORT

A LUCKY LUKE ADVENTURE 19
ON THE DALTONS' TRAIL

A LUCKY LUKE ADVENTURE 20
THE OKLAHOMA LAND RUSH

DECEMBER 2009

A LUCKY LUKE ADVENTURE 21
THE 20TH CAVALRY

FEBRUARY 2010

A LUCKY LUKE ADVENTURE 22
EMPEROR SMITH

APRIL 2010

A LUCKY LUKE ADVENTURE 23
A CURE FOR THE DALTONS

JUNE 2010

A LUCKY LUKE ADVENTURE 24
THE JUDGE

AUGUST 2010

9th CINEBOOK
The 9th Art Publisher
www.cinebook.com

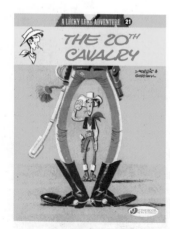